DEATH
OF THE
BLACK-
HAIRED
GIRL

Also by Robert Stone

DEATH
OF THE
BLACK-
HAIRED
GIRL

ROBERT STONE

corsair

Constable & Robinson Ltd
55–56 Russell Square
London WC1B 4HP
www.constablerobinson.com

First published in the United States
by Houghton Mifflin Harcourt, New York, 2013

This edition first published in the UK by Corsair,
an imprint of Constable & Robinson, 2014

Original book design by Brian Moore

This is a work of fiction. Names, characters, places
and incidents are either the product of the author's imagination
or are used fictitiously, and any resemblance to actual persons,
living or dead, or to actual events or locales is entirely coincidental.

A copy of the British Library Cataloguing in
Publication data is available from the British Library

ISBN 978-1-47211-539-3 (B-format paperback)
ISBN 978-1-47211-653-6 (A-format paperback)
ISBN 978-1-47211-540-9 (ebook)

1 3 5 7 9 10 8 6 4 2

Printed and bound in the UK

For Ian

1

"YOU LOOK LIKE A WHITE CAPTIVE," Shelby said to Maud.

Maud saw herself in a mirror on the bathroom door, winter pale, wrapped in a Salish blanket. She pulled the blanket tighter around her thighs and shoulders. Her skin was very fair but rosy after her shower.

"You think?"

"Totally," her roommate said.

Maud huddled beside a bay window of her suite, shivering deliciously in the drafts of ice-edged wind that filtered through the plaster and old stone of the building. Cheerless dawn lit the pinnacles and tracery of the Gothic towers across the Common. One by one, southeast by northwest, the trunks of the elms along the walks lightened to gray. All at once, the street lamps died together.

It was all so bleak and beautiful and she was happy to be there. She loved the morning, loved warming herself against the venerable drafts of Cross Inn, safe from the steely street outside.

She wrapped the blanket more tightly, tossed her hair from side to side. Maud's hair was silky and black as could be; it dazzled against her pale skin, high color and her bluest of eyes. She had always worn it long and would not dream of playing geek with it, uglifying herself with streaks and punky cuts. Sometimes she used an iron on it the way girls in the sixties had. Beautiful was a word Maud heard too often and too early in life. Once, in high school, she had tried to steal an art book from the Metropolitan Museum of Art gift shop because one of her teachers said there was a Whistler painting of a girl who looked like her.

They had stopped her at the top of the steps outside. The store manager herself had followed Maud across the crowded lobby and blocked her escape on the top step and then stood by, trembling with satisfaction, while an officer made her produce the bag from under her parka. Maud had obliged the ugly old bitch by crying, and even five years later she remembered every moment of that mortification, right down to the spring weather and the faces of the dumb tourists who stood nudging each other at the museum doors. She had worried about losing her National Merit Scholarship and about her father finding out, but nothing came of it.

Still attending her mirror, Maud bent her head forward and let her hair hang down in front. She had considered art history as a major but then changed it to English with a writing concentration. She straightened up for the glass. Her neck was shapely and strong.

In front of the church on the edge of the Common, she saw

the homeless men gathered to wait for meal tickets. They huddled like animals, leaking plastic foam from their dumpster ski jackets. A few of them tried to find space to sit on the narrow park rail which, at some time in the eighties, had been set with spikes to discourage unsightly feeding and defecation. A new franchise hotel had its main entrance across the street.

Railings had been reconfigured; a city bus stop was moved a block. There had been protests; there were always timely protests. The protesters accused the parks department of obliging the hotel, catering to consistent bias against the homeless, the handicapped and the poor. Maud had written a witty and passionate column in the college newspaper, opposing and mocking the move which had been much admired. It went without saying that most downtown workers, as well as most students with classes in nearby buildings, felt more comfortable after the work was done. Even Maud had to admit that it had been an ordeal to pass by every day, and there was no question but that the Common looked more cool without the poor.

Outside, the morning rush had not quite begun. A city bus was parked at its last designated stop with its motor running. Traffic was sparse, and only a few late-shift college workmen were headed for the underground parking lot below the Common.

"So, hey," said Maud's roommate, whom everyone called Shell. "What you got on today?"

Shell was an actress and had been a principal in a few independent movie productions of the sort that played limited-release houses. Her name was Shelby Magoffin, and she came originally from eastern Kentucky. She talked that talk as necessary but had many voices. She was studying for a degree in drama, having transcended her hard upbringing and a much too early marriage. Shell was not one of your extremely pretty actresses but she was memorable, thin and eccentric in a way that would have brought her character roles in the old Hollywood. Sometimes people asked her about her marriage — other students, curious. "Ever hear from the guy?"

"Oh," Shell would say, "first boy I loved," quoting the Judy Collins song.

"No," she would tell them, "never." But that was not true. He called her sometimes.

"You got a date with Mister Man today?" Shell asked.

"Early appointment," Maud told her.

She folded her hair under a black sailor's watch cap, borrowed a hooded jacket of Shell's, put on painter's pants and hiking boots. She had on nice underwear, though, in case, as her mother had always said, she was hit by a bus or, as Mom omitted to say, overcome by passion.

They took a shortcut past the church, now sounding its seven o'clock chimes. Their route would take her past the bus stop and the queue of bums, but Maud felt it would be craven and unprincipled to avoid it.

The early morning rush hour was beginning as the two women hit Amity Street. A few pedestrians walked quickly toward the college and the office buildings on the far side of the Common. Cars were caught at the light, and the healthier, more aggressive among the poor, mainly young black men who had taken places at the front of the line, stepped into traffic, talking.

"Yo, I say, Cadillac man."

But the drivers were not Cadillac men, or if they had Cadillacs, the Cadillacs were twelve years old and patched, and plenty of the drivers were women. At that hour, Cadillac men would not appear, although at ten there would be plenty, and Saab sahibs and Bimmers, thoughtful Volvo men and suburban soubrettes in armored Abrams-class deuce-and-a-half Windstars or Jeep personal-use vehicles. So there was agitation and the locking of retro car doors, dirty looks from the honest working stiffs and silent muttering behind the rolled-up windows. Out walking from the city garage, older men put their hands in their pockets and kept their eyes on the street. Young white men in bunches laughed it off, red-faced, simmering with piss-off. The panhandlers laughed back at them, hot-eyed, selling wolf tickets.

There had actually been a summit the previous year — the City, the College, the Police, the Coalition for the Homeless and the Overseers of the Common. Participants in the summit were cautioned against the use of certain words. The words: dirtbag, wino, bum, scum, street scum, chronic nuisance, predator, freeloader, disenfranchised, disadvantaged, the poor, criminal, jailbird, vagrant. Biculturally conscious, the summit included the words *cabrón,* criminal, *ratón, ladrón.* The mayor, free on bail after his arrest and indictment for racketeering, gave a comment to the struggling newspaper of record to set in funny-colored inks.

"This is talk we don't want to hear in our city," said his worship the mayor.

The panhandlers watched the two women go by; a few affected haughty indifference. Shelby was dimmed down in a checkered lumber jacket and wraparound Oakleys of a midnight hue. Maud, in the flat-soled hiking boots, was just under six feet tall; she towered over Shelby when they walked together, though there were plenty of girls at the college who were taller than Maud. The female students, mainly teenagers, were on average taller than the men of the town.

Steely wind hit them from the bay, a few blocks beyond the Common. Cross Inn was on a corner where marine gales coming up the river were set spinning by a cluster of high-rise bank and insurance company buildings. They whipped all winter through the Gothic courtyards of Old Campus on the other side of the Common. Beyond the colleges and the ghettos of Shoreham and Northwell stood the high ridge that showed seasons to the grimy town. In winter it displayed bare rock, dead leaves, brown branches, streaky snow. God had raised the ridge centuries before to protect the colony and the college from the pagan and papist savages on the other side. The college had always required and received protection.

Maud, a city girl to the marrow, had hardly noticed the ridge at first. She knew it was dangerous to jog up there. But Shell,

who was a mountain girl—"a mountain grill," she liked to say—
would declare obeisance each time she went out by way of Cross
Street.

"I will lift up mine eyes unto the hills, from whence cometh
my help," she would say. Of course it was a joke, one of Shell's
jokes on herself, on her people and their God. Once during
their freshman orientation nature walk, Shell had halted two
steps from the sunning spot of an eastern banded timber rattler, which woke and raised itself, slithered sidewise and stood
its ground. Its tail disappeared in a blur of speed and reptile
rhythms, clackety-rap. Its eyes were all business.

Maud, a few feet behind her new friend, saw the thing, called
out, "Oh, shit! Oh, Shell!" Maud thought Shelby Magoffin was
like a seashell, pink and fragile. Sometimes Maud teased her
with the name. "Seashell, watch it!"

The male upperclassman leading the walk had lifted Shell up
by the elbows and swung her out of striking range. "Asshole,"
Shell had muttered ungratefully.

"Ever see a big old rattler before, Shell?" the earthy-crunchy
youth had asked.

"Only in church," Shell had told him.

The other freshmen had taken it in. They had also registered
Maud's New Yorky swearing. And Shell's cool answer—they
knew it was a cool answer whether or not they caught the reference to Pentecostal snake handling. And Shell Magoffin was
forever Seashell, though the origins of the name and its significance were left unclear. Later, as the other students came to

understand that she was an actor in the sorts of movies they went to see, they realized that the goofy name was part of it.

On Cross Street the panhandlers did not usually hit on Maud or her friends. In fact they rarely hit on any of the particularly attractive girls. Where raillery might be expected, there was none; no teasing between the lost boys and the college girls. There was too much privilege and anger — a terrifying atavistic cloud enfolding shame and resentment, even humiliation and murder. Bad things had happened. Everyone knew better.

That morning Maud and Shell found themselves headed the same way. At Stoddard Street they followed the Common past Hale Gate, joined now by kids on their way to the day's first class.

"You don't have a class," Shell said to her friend. "How come you're up so early?"

"Date for coffee."

"With him?" Without waiting for an answer, Shell told Maud, "I have rehearsals until after nine. I could sleep away tonight." Shell looked at her with wry sympathy.

"Thanks, friend. He's not free tonight."

"I was gonna say," Shell said, "but I didn't."

Snow began to fall, although it seemed too cold for snow. "Anyway, this is just an appointment," Maud said.

They kept their heads down, making for Bay's, the nearest coffee place to campus.

"Bringing him coffee?"

"Yeah, right," Maud said. "Cold coffee date."

"Older guys are so much better," Shell teased. "They, like, know so much more."

Shell's celebrated career had already brought her into close contact with putative adults. Some of them were very famous and said to be very powerful, but she was not impressed.

Bay's coffee shop operated on the ground floor of a four-story converted office building that had become a halfway house for deinstitutionalized mental patients. The halfway-house people had made a headquarters of the place and gathered there from daybreak until seven in the evening. Bay's kept chairs outside for them, which they occupied in every weather. All day they predominated; their behavior and queer psychic emanations gave the coffee shop an unsettling spin. A stranger sitting down for an espresso would presently notice another customer's peculiar intensity, an overloud conversation punctuated by excessive laughter or the imminent lunacy of a silence. An inappropriate emotional tone prevailed. Some people liked it — art students and Shell Magoffin. It gave Maud the creeps, but she wanted some coffee. She followed Shell across the brick plaza.

The mentally ill customers were known as Housies or Outmates. At times, terrace chairs would become vacant — say, when the Outmates had made up a posse to go shopping at the nearest Safeway, four scary inner-city blocks away. Shopping alone or in twos, they might be confronted or even physically abused by anyone from the younger of the homeless to the police. In the vertical society of that city, the Outmates' standing was low. They were unpopular and somewhat defenseless. No one believed the things they said, so their complaints were dismissible. Streets on which the coeds walked confidently held dangers for the halfway-housed. It seemed that only the tough female mounted troopers were nice to them, knowing their names and letting them pet their mounts, like children. The mounted policewomen also treated the halfway-house residents' leader, Herbert, with a reserved, humorous respect. Herbert had become the residents' leader by virtue of his very loud voice and broad general knowledge.

As the girls turned into Bay's, Herbert was at his usual table, actively facing down the coming storm. Herbert was the one male habitué who by his assumed right and custom always talked to the girls. "Hey, Shell!" he said at the top of his voice. "Seashell!"

Shell gave him a smile and a pat on the shoulder. Maud's polite smile might have concealed her disgust from most people but did not fool Herbert.

At the coffee counter Maud and Shell asked for the specials of the day to go. Maud bought two *largos,* served by a beautiful young man from Spain, a graduate music student with bleached hair and a row of three earrings. Then the two girls made their way through the shivering halfway-house crowd to the street. Herbert was reading aloud from the local paper, quoting a story on the mayor's legal troubles. There was no one around to listen; the wind increased.

Shell and Maud went different ways. Herbert looked up from his paper to oversee them.

"Hey, have fun, girls!" Herbert called after them. "Bless this world and all who sail in her." He put a hand in his lap and watched them disappear into the first heavy flakes of the storm.

At the gate of Peabody Quad, Maud stopped and set the two coffees down on the cold slate sidewalk. It was time for her to fish out her ID card, which would open the electric lock on the college gate. Once through the gate, it required the opening of three more locks to reach the room where she was headed.

Ever since the first Indian hatchet lodged its blade in the college's single stout oak door during the Seven Years' War, doors and access within had been significant there. For years the place rested behind no more bolts than the resort of young gentry required in any rough-handed New England mill town. Then the sixties struck, with coeducation and power to the people — all sorts of people — and there had even been a solitary unisex bathroom, which languished amid the embarrassment hardly a year after its building, and there was the Throwing Open of the Gates, the Unbolting of the Great Doors, the Opening to the Community. What ensued, drug-wise, crime-wise and in terms of bitterness between the college and the town, was brief but ugly. The opening forth was followed by a locking up, down and sideways that had locksmiths laboring day and night, and now there were three or four doors for everything — even clerks' offices were secured, and elderly dons retired because they spent half their working days trying to distinguish in a dour economy of light which of the cards or keys on their chains opened their outermost office door, which the second, which the third and so on. The coffee Maud had brought cooled on the cold stone while she knelt fiddling and jingling at Professor Brookman's door.

2

STEVEN BROOKMAN HAD a particularly comfortable office in the oldest college building, Cortland Hall. There was a Persian carpet on the floor. The captain's chairs, like the leaded bay windows, were inscribed with the institution's motto: *Lux in umbras procedet.* The phrase referred to the college's ancient determination to confront Algonquians with the prospect of eternal fire.

On Brookman's desk were piled the student assignments due to be graded and returned the following day. He had been awake all of the previous night evading any responsibility to them. Now they were neatly stacked against him on his green college blotter and there seemed nothing for it but to read them. He felt, on that particular morning, that he would rather die.

It was true that most of the papers were fairly boring, but that was not Brookman's problem. The real trouble was that they could be quite ingenious, experimental in style, original or contrarian in reasoning. These were kids whose high school teachers carried them to the airport on their shoulders — the preppie stars, the advanced-placement-class brains and scholar athletes, the alpha girls, the youths of destiny to be raised up or broken by time's wheel. Some schools were said to instruct their students on the techniques for ruling the world. A revered visionary of the nineteenth century had said Brookman's college thought of itself as examining the moral authority of privilege, which was far more high-minded, and exactly the same thing.

He had been hearing Andean flutes outside since dawn, thin wintry sounds just the near side of tonality. The music had become a daily presence around the college. When he picked a paper from the top, whose should it be but young Maud Stack's. It had not been on the pile the day before, from which he had to conclude that she had let herself into the building and his office, to which he had rashly given her a key the year before. Maybe, he thought, he could have the office lock changed, discreetly, at his own expense. An odd guilty thought, of uncharacteristic foreboding.

Maud's paper was too long as usual and also a week late. Maud's assignments were always late. She turned in less than half of the minimum due, invariably borne on one of her fits of manic energy and insight. The results could be truly dazzling. Even on days when he was not particularly in the mood for Maud, he would take up one of her essays with a stirring of anticipation not untouched by dread. Dread of her winning her way inside him again, of threatening to crowd out the contoured life he had made himself, the devotions and sacred loyalties within it.

The student papers that day concerned Marlowe's *Doctor Faustus*. Maud had no line on it; the bookish kids never did. It was low showbiz, they thought; it was vulgar and corny.

The passage that had caught her attention was the one in which the Doctor asks Mephistopheles how he manages to wander about tempting obsessed intellectuals while doing time in hell.

"Why this is hell," says the Diabolus, "nor am I out of it."

"Shakespeare," Maud had written, "would never be so impious."

Next to her line, Brookman wrote: "True."

This is the line that gets to her, an odd precocious insight for a spoiled college girl. In discussion, he will tell her this, if not in so many words.

Maud was seriously, determinedly in love with him. Too young to know better, he would have joked, had it been a joking matter. Which it was not, because that was the situation. She actually *was* too young to know better.

Maud was a passionate person; Brookman also. He was not immune to obsession, which was really the basis of his success as a travel and adventure writer. He had been crazy about Maud for a year, not only because she was beautiful and sexually inspired but because of her youth, her moments of sheer brilliance, the unquiet being behind her eyes.

Not that the flame burned less brightly now but that the kindling furnished a different smoke. As far as Maud went, he would have to digest the venom of loss. There was only one love the loss of which he could not contemplate, and it was not Maud's. A few days before, Brookman's wife of eleven years had, with confidence and joy, confirmed to him that she was pregnant. She was on leave for the semester and had been in Saskatchewan on her family's farm since Canadian Thanksgiving, their ten-year-old daughter along, leaving Brookman to his ways. He loved her very much and was filled with guilt and superstitious dread about their safety. He had resolved to break off the thing with Maud. Whatever it took.

Brookman walked from his desk to the Tudor windows that opened to the quad. He brushed open the gray and black curtains, which displayed the same salvific motto of missionary days, about darkness and light and converting the Indians. His desk was genuinely old, a rolltop bequeathed to the college by Charles Sanders Peirce or some other Brahmin savant of the nineteenth century.

Outside in the quad he saw a middle-aged man walking deliberately in the direction of the street gate, one of the lost souls who wandered the campus yards and passages at every hour. The security staff knew all the regulars and, even in the aftermath of the World Trade Center events scarcely three years before, let them have free range of the place. Art students who could make them sit still liked to pose such people. They had faces undergraduates would recall all their lives, not remembering who they were, where or when seen. Maybe, Brookman thought, Maud had one of them in mind, locating Faustus already in hell. Was it not an odd line for an adolescent to seize on — the world as hell? Not really. Father's influence. Her father had been a New York City police detective. Her mother, dead.

The man Brookman watched was in his forties and had been around the college for a very long time. He lived in the small downtown condo his parents had bought for him. No backpacks for him; along with the plastic bags from Price Chopper and Target and 7-Eleven he carried a worn briefcase with a college sticker he had pasted on it more than twenty years before as a student. Sometimes he walked silently, eyes fixed on the pavement. At other times he carried on a dialogue with the unseen, an exchange that sounded so nuanced and literate that new students and faculty thought he was addressing them or talking into a cell phone. Occasionally he grew angry and shouted a bit, but like many of the delusional, he had learned not to confront real people who — downtown — could prove all too substantial.

Brookman stayed at the window to watch him. It was possible to picture this man sitting all night in the room his family had bought for him, and Brookman wondered if he was alone or accompanied through the small hours by the voices he heard. Whether he turned on the light or sat in the dark with them, whether they were visible to him or simply voices. What their identities were, how they treated him. Did they make him angry? Certainly he heard no good news from them.

Sometimes the man wandered into the college buildings and rode the elevators. Security never stopped him; no one bothered him. If he was in an elevator when someone got on, he would get off, even if he had just got on. If he was trapped in the elevator by a crowd, he began to act desperately sane, polishing his glasses with his handkerchief, nodding pleasantly at no one in particular, ignoring his voices. When he reached a floor he would race out, plainly agitated. Madness was hardly unknown in the college. There were others like this man, forever groping through the maze of alma mater.

Still at the window, Brookman watched the quad. The only color was of the autumn-yellowed grass on the lawns; the sky matched the sidewalks and the Norman tower of New Chapel. There was faint snow, salting a drizzle. It was slightly cheering because the month had been gray and wet, more chill than truly cold.

He saw that the man with the bags had reversed direction. The man was now walking as fast as he could, fleeing a noisy group of students excited by the powdering of snow. He was dull-eyed, chin down, jaw clenched. He didn't like the snow on his fair balding skull, didn't like the happy youths. In a moment he would turn again and walk back to his own voices. It was so much work to be crazy, Brookman thought.

There sounded a knock against the dark paneling of Brookman's office door, a loud single rap followed by a pause, then two rapid knocks. It was a d-delta in toneless Morse code, a little of Brookman's obsolete nautical education that he had passed on to Maud, an impractical skill for some decades but useful at that moment.

Tiny snowflakes rested on the locks of her hair that showed around the edges of her watch cap. Brookman took a quick look

right and left along the hall. Maud noticed his display of guilty
stealth. She brushed back the hood she wore over the cap and
laughed at him. He drew her into the room, gathering her up by
her jacket and yanking her, somewhat violently, into his office.
The containers of cold coffee at her feet went over.

"Help," she said.

"If you don't mind," he said, walking to the inlaid window to
close the dusty curtains. *Lux in umbras procedet.* Then he kissed
her and found himself in his Maud transport. He felt as if he
could drain her, overwhelm and consume her, all her scents and
silky turns, the firm athlete's body. Or else that he was the one
being consumed, confused and incapable of escape.

"Oh," she said, "you're hard."

"Don't be coarse," he said. It had taken him a moment to get
the reference. She didn't care for this reproach.

"Coarse. What?" She demanded an answer of him in the agitated adolescent manner of the time. "You think that's coarse?
You're such a middle-class prude."

"Working-class prude." He had been around the world at
least once and had never thought of himself as a prude. "Maybe
just lower class."

Before long he was sitting at his desk and she was more or less
under it, down on him, and he could only think of those long
lips and those all-at-once — on a single day it seemed — suddenly knowing eyes. He bent to twist her long black silky hair
into a coil and ran his fingers, wrapped in it, down the back of
her neck.

He sat in a dazzled aftermath, watching her every move. She brazenly blew him a kiss, lips to fingers.

"Oh, baby" was all he could think of to say.

Not poetry. Perhaps inappropriate? Certainly not the older-brotherly chat he had had in mind for this particular visit.

"I love you," she said. "I love your brains and cock and knees and eyes. I love your hokey dipshit tattoos. I don't scare and you don't scare, but I'm shit terrified that I so adore your bones, Professor Brookman. Aren't you scared of loving me?"

"Maybe I don't love you, Maud. Maybe I'm just obsessed with you, body and soul."

"Now," she said, "you're scaring me."

"What we have is fearsome. We're both going to live in dread." He saw that she was at the point of tears.

"But," she said, "with your wife, with that shepherdess creature, the Albigensian or whatever — that's all cozy sweetness and light, right?"

"That's right. But you're a little tart. A little Kerry gallows bird of an outlaw. Maybe we'll swing on a rope in the rain for each other."

She put a lock on him, held him as hard as she could. She was trembling.

"You're scaring me, Steve."

"Because I love you," he said. Yet love was not really what he felt for her. In times to come he would long ponder what he had been trying to say.

"I thought what you said about Shakespeare and Marlowe

was on the money," Brookman told her when all was in order. "Faustus and hell and so on. Well observed."

"Think I'm right?"

"I do."

"Why?"

"You tell me why," Brookman said.

"Because Shakespeare would never have said the world was hell. It would have been blasphemous."

"Shakespeare made some defamatory statements about the world."

"Yeah. But he wouldn't have Mephisto be right. Not with hell right there. They both know a single drop of Christ's blood could save him."

"What a wicked creature you are," Brookman said. "Get out. What are you doing here anyway?"

"I want to see you. Is your wife, like . . . ?"

Brookman's wife and daughter were returning early to keep their Christmas at home with him. Ellie's parents were of a Mennonite sect that more or less rejected Christmas, but they still expected a winter visit from their daughter and grandchild. Watching Maud, Brookman saw a cloud of resentment cross her brow. She did not like hearing about his domestic arrangements.

He cut her off.

"We don't know yet when she can get back. There's a storm in western Canada. Planes may not fly. On the other hand, they may."

"But I want to see you."

"We'll see each other."

"I'll call you later, Steve," she said. "Have to buy a pretzel and get to class."

When she was out the door, he went to the window, drew the curtains open again and watched her walk across the quad. Frozen rain clung to the coats of students passing by. The man Brookman had seen earlier was standing by the street gate, staring at Maud as she passed.

He closed his heraldic curtains again and turned out the lights. Such domesticities served to bring Maud closer to him, because that was what he did when she came to his office outside of hours.

Brookman's appointments were about to begin, and he wanted a break between the stream of Maud's frantic consciousness and his first actual student of the day. He kicked his rolling chair back against the wall and put his feet up. The room was still scented with Maud's perfume and the soapy schoolgirl odors of her body, and Brookman found it difficult to banish her from his mind.

3

CROSS INN, WHERE Maud and Shell lived, afforded beautiful views of city and campus. In the twenties and thirties it had been the best hotel in town. Over time, like everything else downtown, it degenerated, eventually becoming a ratty dope-and-suicide hotel. In the end, the college acquired and renovated it for a dormitory, keeping some of the art nouveau pieces and paneling of the original. To Shell it still looked depressing. She liked to say that the place accommodated as much dope and nearly as many suicides as a dorm as it had as a welfare hotel. This was an exaggeration. But the dim-lit hallways, dusty mirrors and portraits of scholarly immortals were, Shell thought, a bringdown. She knew a cheapo hotel when she saw one. One tip-off was the smell of insecticide and garbage awaiting incineration. Shell and her mother had lived for a while in a welfare motel on the edge of a river running brown across from a stretch of woodland.

On her way back from her poetry class, Shell had gotten a call on her cell phone from her ex-husband, John Clammer. She promptly switched it off. Then he called her on the college's automated service line. It seemed humiliating to go through the business of taking the phone off the hook and trying to ignore the cacophony and wanga-wanga that would ensue. And she would be goddamned if Crazy John Clammer would drive her into the cold weather.

Shell had a restraining order against her ex, but it seemed to provide no practical release from his phone calls. In any case, when he referred to it, he tended to laugh in a way she found unpleasant. To actualize the legal abstraction, Shell had purchased a Sauer Luftwaffe-style automatic pistol, which she kept on her knee during Crazy John's phone calls to remind her of the syllogism that stated all men were mortal.

"Hello," she said sweetly in one of the British accents she had been learning on tape for an audition piece.

"Ma'am," said Crazy John, "may I please speak with Miss Shelby Magoffin?"

"That," Shelby said, "is forbidden, I'm afraid."

"Forbidden?"

"Hello, John. You ain't supposed to telephone me. Send a e-mail."

"Shelby? Honey?"

"How come you're being affectionate? I thought you hated my poor guts. You said that."

"I thought you wanted a real man. I wasn't gonna hurt you."

"Don't you treat me like I'm your little girl punk, Johnny.

Don't think I can't get you arrested from up here. When you gonna grow up?"

Shelby was subject to goofy telephone calls at the college, and not only from her ex. For the most part she slipped under the radar of C-list paparazzi, but the year before she had made a screamer called *The Harrowing of Hell,* and since then she got calls from admirers who told her they liked imagining her dead in various costumes and wanted a date. Her agent had provided her with a "personal-representative number" to dead-letter such calls, but no matter how often she changed numbers the bastards seemed to slip through, and Crazy John too. The calls weren't frequent but, depending on her mood, they imposed a certain gloom.

"Remember when you said I was a good man?" John asked.

"Oh, you are a good man, Johnny. It's just"—she thought of what it might be with Crazy John—"it's just your ways are not my ways. And my ways are not your ways and the center will not hold and the past is forever past and . . . you know, man. Leave me alone, will ya?"

She had been warned about John Clammer back home. He had been older than she—as it turned out, older by nearly ten years. He was crazy too, inasmuch as he and his family struggled a lot with emotional illness. But he was gorgeous to look at, especially for sixteen-year-old Shell. He sang and looked like one of God's personal sunbeam angels. He had curly black hair and rosy cheeks and a nose that turned up to show more of his nostrils than you regularly saw of someone's, and—don't ask why—she thought that was cute too. She believed, in her teenage years, that he looked and sang so like an angel he might actually be one. He played the guitar and sang in church and when he spoke regular words his voice was joyous and delightsome. In fact, some boys from Middleboro let him pay to make a prayer CD called *Worship for the Challenged in Vision.* He had his and Shell's picture on it, showing them in prayer with their eyes closed, but when you tried to play it, it didn't, and when he reached the boys in Middleboro, they told him only blind people could hear it. John had paid them $150. Still, never knew though, but that picture of her on the CD might have led to great subsequent success. For her, not for him.

Because as Shell grew older and John got crazier, Shell persuaded her mother, who had started as an online psychic and graduated as a psychiatric nurse, to get John Clammer confined. Then Shell's life changed. She became an actress and went off to the college in Amesbury, which he called Hell House.

John's hope was that she be saved and they perform Christian music together. Shell's hope was that a stone be tied around John's neck and he be cast into the depths of the sea. It was John's equally crazy but well-spoken aunt Calla Lily who made them get married. A dreadful idea.

"You yourself told me I was a good man," John whined to Shelby on the phone. "I can sing and we'll pray together."

"Jesus Christ," said Shell. "Please, John."

"Look, I'll forgive you," John said. "Just let me take you home."

Best not to mention the restraining order, she thought. But she was losing patience.

"I forgive you too, Johnny. Just . . . let me have my life."

Crazy John scorned her new life. When he began to tell her about his new job, she rather lost it. It was a damn good job too, in Boone National Forest, he said.

"Doin' what, John? Cooking crank? Cutting up bear bladders? Poaching ginseng? Growing dope? Ain't you too old for that shit?"

Not that he was capable of any of it. The methmeisters considered him a snitch and a thief. He couldn't tell ginseng from poison ivy (you could trust her on that). He didn't have the wherewithal to maintain a weed crop. And a bear would have *his* bladder for lunch before John found the safety on a Mossberg.

"You're a damn bitch, ain't you?" John asked. "Fuckin' little bitch movie whore, ain't you?"

"Now John," she said, "that's unfair. John, listen to me. Do you know what a Personal Threat Assessment Team is?"

"What is it?"

"A Personal Threat Assessment Team is a security force the industry provides. They're monitoring our conversation now. If you persist, I'll have to ask them to step in."

She took advantage of the ensuing silence to hang up.

Thankfully he did not call back. While she was at the computer, she e-mailed her mother in Whitesville. Her mom didn't care for her much but always wanted to go to the festival at

Sundance when Shell was featured. Mom had become a nurse, raising herself in the world. She had never talked to Shell from one year to the next until the two films came out, the first one at Sundance.

> MOM HOWARU JCLAMMER STILL LOCKED UP?
> KEEP ME INFORMED HEAR?

Shell did not like e-mail. She always felt there was someone listening, reading. She trusted the telephone more, even to buy weed. For all she knew John Clammer might somehow be out there. He was timid but clever and resourceful in a way.

Her mother got back to her in half an hour, as she had taken to doing of late.

> HONEYBUNCH JC GOT TOOK TO THE ART
> SHOP TO PAINT PLATES THIS MORNING AND
> HE COME BACK WITH THE BUS. HE'S NOT
> SUPPOSED TO HAVE HIS CELL PHONE BUT
> THEY USE OTHER PEOPLE'S. FONDEST LOVE
> MOM.

Fondest love, Shell thought. Right, I'm fine, Mom. She made a mental note to ask John for one of his painted plates. A religious one might be nice. God Bless Our Happy Home, maybe. She might give it to Maud for Christmas.

4

LEAVING BROOKMAN'S OFFICE, Maud bought herself a pretzel with mustard and headed for her art history class in the Fefferman Museum. The figure that held her fast through the hour, although it was not the figure under discussion, was the sculpted waltz in which Rodin positioned himself and Camille Claudel. She knew nothing of the story. Whenever she looked at it — as she did often — she saw the two of them there, herself and Brookman.

The shortest route back to Cross led her past Whelan Hospital and the crowds that demonstrated in front of the women's center at the obstetrics clinic there. Whelan performed the abortions that the town's bigger hospital, religiously affiliated, declined to do.

When she was first a student at the college, Maud tried going to Mass at one of the local churches, Our Lady of Fátima. Maybe she appeared a little hippieish. Anyway, she had never felt warmly welcomed. Also the Fátima story, about the children and the prophecies, embarrassed her. She turned away from church, and as the years passed the Friday crowds in front of Whelan annoyed Maud more and more.

The demonstrators were elderly, mostly female Catholics, old-time Catholics. Maud told people that they reminded her of her mother, which was completely untrue because her mother had aspired to gentility, was not very religious and would never have demonstrated against anything. In Amesbury, the right-to-life issue was decidedly a class thing. Over in nearby Connecticut, the family-planning movement had been all but founded and funded because a hundred years ago the Bush family had felt there were too many Italians in Bridgeport.

There were a few men among the marchers, mainly older, wearing imperfects discounted at the mall, looking as though they had just come from the slot machines at the nearest low-rent casino. People smoked.

Some of the women protesters had a few pale hardscrabble children with them and carried signs that read STOP THE MURDERS, GOD IS LOVE and SAVE GOD'S ANGELS. Others carried more aggressive placards: DEATH TO THE HATERS OF LIFE; ROME FELL THROUGH FOUL ABORTION, OUR COUNTRY WILL TOO; WHORES WILL DIE OF THEIR SIN. They somehow drew onlookers' attention to the crazies in the crowd, who seemed as if they'd grown close to Jesus the hard way.

Maud, newly an editor of the college's *Gazette,* wanted to strike against the harassment at Whelan. What infuriated her most were the pictures of terminated fetuses a few of the demonstrators carried. Maud had a plan to deal with their piety, make them eat their miraculous chain letters to Saint Jude and the pictures their potbellied epicene prelates and blow-dried chiseling preachers had assembled. She would write an article for the *Gazette,* and she too would collect pictures to include with it. These pictures were as genuinely moving and heartbreaking as the others, though they bespoke a different point of view. Maud thought them an answer to the murdered cute kids' photos.

Maud was still outside the hospital entrance when she ran into Jo Carr, an ex-nun who worked in the college counseling office. They had been friendly two years before but rarely saw each other now.

"Hey, Maud," Jo called to her. "Come help us out! We can use some candy stripers on the wards."

"If I ever have time, Jo. Maybe."

"Time," Jo said. "They don't give you much, I know." She looked at the grim procession of pro-lifers. She would not have included life on their list of things to cheer for. "Gonna write about these demonstrators?"

"Wait and see," Maud told her.

Jo shook her head. "Don't be cruel!"

"Cruel!" Maud half shouted. Jo hurried to disengage as she walked down the hill.

"The wrong side has feelings too, kid."

What Maud really wanted to do was see Brookman, but she elected to go swimming instead. When she got back to Cross to get her pool gear, the place was empty. Shell had gone out for fencing practice, which, along with the gymnastics and the enunciation lessons, was part of the highly regarded theater course at the college. Maud grabbed a change of lingerie and a clean denim shirt for after-swim, her own clothes this time.

It had started to snow lightly again by the time she got to the gym. It was called the Biedler Athletic Center, after the grain millionaire who paid for it, a brick modernist building showing lots of glass and built into a low hillside. Through the dark winter evening, in the exciting whirl of snowflakes, its lighted windows were welcoming, promising warmth and invigoration beyond them. The gym had a huge lobby with overhead and floor lights. At the entrance, a blond basketball giant with a bony Slavic face checked her college ID.

She could hear shouts, grunts, stomps, the smash of rubber balls against hardwood floors, the sounds echoing down tiled hallways but muted by the resilient walls. Somewhere in this building Shell was practicing her swordswomanship, and Maud, who had never seen her at it, wanted a look. She went down corridors peering through the small windows in the doors until, on the second floor, she found Shell in her mask and whites, engaging a shorter, chunky girl with close-cropped hair. Maud watched through the rectangular window. Shell's opponent was standing her ground in what apparently was the classic position, parrying Shell's thrusts. Shell looked skittery and a lot less expert but Maud could hear her little yelps when she leaned into an attack. It was fun to watch but embarrassing to see her roommate being defeated.

The water in the pool downstairs was cold. A few lanes were free because of the weather outside; only the dedicated swimmers were there. The funny thing about swimming, Maud reflected, was that counting laps to make the mile distance absorbed your consciousness so that you thought about the count even when the crawl stroke was the farthest thing from your mind. This, she knew, was an upside; it was boring but peaceful, and it strengthened her resolve in what she was about to do. After the laps she took a hot shower, toweled off and dried her hair. The few other girls in the locker room were aware of her.

Walking across downtown from the Common, Maud had the sleety snow at her back. From the practice fields half a mile away she could make out the players' voices. One of the sports teams, weather or not. The old seminary buildings were past what was once the thriving factory district of Amesbury. The area was more prosperous than in years before, but it was still shabby. Along the curbs of Camp Street stood ridges of soiled snow refrozen after a thaw, being layered over once again by the falling flakes. There was black ice scarred with skid marks near the curb and frozen dead leaves that clogged the street's drains, peeled rubber in the gutter, blackened chunks of tailpipe, wands of aluminum siding. The last block was across an overpass spanning the railroad tracks. An art gallery and an Ethiopian restaurant occupied the street level of a two-story building that leaned against the seminary.

Maud cut across the small quad where the *Gazette* lived and saw lights on. People stood just inside the door, out of the cold. She wanted the office to herself to get the job done. She walked out to the main street of town and went into Downey's to nurse a beer at a table. It was a bar where most students didn't go, a sort of townie bar. She was perfectly at home there unless some drunk hit on her. She was resolved not to let herself be swept into some scene or other. It was a night for serious business.

The tired waitress knew her.

"Hi, sweetie." The woman lowered her voice. "No date tonight?"

Maud smiled. "Late date."

From Downey's, March Street took her to the falls, where the river that meandered deliberately along the edge of the Common coiled itself into the force that had long before spun a hundred wheels to make sailcloth for long-gone coasters. This was the far end of the old waterfront, the ungentrified part that never lent itself to any more development than a few microbreweries and loft sweatshops. Wheels here didn't grind out anything but hard time for the poorest illegals in peonage, or the afternoons of young weight-watcher moms pedaling to music videos.

At the far side of the bridge, the corners were ruled by gangbangers preparing for their prison time, in hoodies, pants low. The street talk was lame now, left to professional rappers; the

Spanish was without color; the English was groping. What they knew the ghetto kids couldn't say. What they said came out of streaming media and not from the dead streets. People who followed such things — among them grad students in sociology — said the small children in the old wooden tenements that Norman Rockwell liked to people with his folk didn't know jump-rope rhymes anymore, couldn't play stickball or hopscotch or choose up sides going one potato two potato. In summer the basketball courts were empty. Grandma weighs ninety pounds, she's on crack, mom's a slave or turning tricks at interstate rest areas, adolescent dad's working on his prison tats or wearing curlers for his roomie. All the graffiti is black.

Some might have thought that the two parts of the city — Maple Park the poor townie side and the college-Common area — didn't intersect, but they did. Heroin had found a niche on both banks of the Mill River, its glint detectable to the aware in such unlikely realms as fashion photography. Models were as lean as ever and also conveyed a quality of anxious personal drama. Junkie chic had not disappeared and heroin still outsold cocaine.

So the college students found their way into hard drugs. Some of them had contacts in the medical school. More took the walk down toward the river where it crossed the March Street Bridge. Maud knew the drill; it had been demonstrated to her a week or two earlier by one who knew all too well. After dark, customers from the college side of the bridge brought money in a white athletic sock and tied it to the bridge's handrail. They then proceeded to the far side of the bridge, where stood a small bodega. If they chose, they could buy a Red Bull or a Lifewater. When they recrossed the bridge, they would find a replacement for the original sock which contained what they were trying to buy. This sort of thing had had repercussions, in both college and town, but it seemed still to be thriving.

Maud was not a user but an ambitious journalist, and she had made a previous reconnoitering trip accompanied by a some-time-user girlfriend to witness the procedure. Her intention was to do the heroin story with anonymous interviews when she was finished with right-to-lifing exhibitionists and their gallery of holy innocents. On her last outing she secretly photographed a buy.

Surely there would be someone here who might appreciate a bag or a sale on this night of punishing snow and hail, but there was no action on the bridge. The inboard rail showed its single graffito, a black-and-white puffy cloud — maybe a stylized expressionist sock — and the printed polychrome Day-Glo letters TARD. It was never certain whether tags were left by street kids or art students. Underneath, the cars splashed through toward the suburbs.

At the *Gazette* office sometime later, she set out to do the first draft of the piece she had in mind. She eyed the computer screen with a small smile, slid into a comfortable slouch in her chair and wrote what she had planned. "Christ Scientist?" it opened. "No offense intended to the friends of Eddy, with their unspeakably humongous empty domes and morgue-like reading rooms. Nor to the denizens of megachurches nor of the Holy Romantic Megachurch itself. However, how about a little offense to the jolly band of folks who treat us to those cute-kid pictures of fetuses fifty times a year?"

In the next two columns she inserted two photographs from a text called *Smith's Recognizable Patterns of Human Malformation*. The pictures in it were of live births, newborns delivered into the breathing world. They were Maud's counter to the heartwarming fetuses. The first was a photograph of a baby born with hydrolethalus syndrome. It seemed about one-third head. In the color photograph it was eyeless, and its mouth consisted of no more than a tragic moue. Science had identified the chromosomal roots of this condition. Children born with the disorder lived for as long as a day.

Beside this baby was a photograph of an infant with Meckel-Gruber syndrome. Babies born with this disorder look preternaturally old. Carriers of the gene that bears it are genetically unrecognizable.

Maud's text continued:

> They say that the Assembly of God, assembled by
> God (sort of like the Queen's Own Fusiliers), treats
> us to the spectacle of eternal punishment in a kind of
> haunted house acted out by whooped-up teenagers
> called Hell House. This is a sort of fun-terrifying
> spectacle, like a life-size diorama out of Dante or

Hieronymus Bosch but much dumber, where you
follow the host through a squeaky door into scenes
of unending torment presented to you by Christ
Torturer the Lord of Unending Piss-Off. This
personage is watching your every move for an excuse
to fry your ass, not just for an hour, not just for a year,
but always. Always.

He's the only Son of his divine dad, God
Abortionist. Who's your daddy?! Yes, friends, twenty
percent of pregnancies spontaneously abort. And lots
of those that don't aren't nearly as lovable as the ones
in the signs right-to-lifers carry.

These paragraphs were illuminated by two more listings from
Smith's. In one, it seemed some wag had placed little striped hats
on the angular, bony victims of Beals-Hecht syndrome. Across
the page from these was a creature brought to term though
suffering from early urethral obstruction sequence, or "prune
belly."

"So, folks," Maud went on, "see how the great Imaginary
Paperweight in the Vast Eternal Blue has all his little ones cov-
ered, so let's make sure they join us. There's life after birth!
That's what jails and lethal injections are for!"

Afterward she walked the late streets. Flakes hurled around
her until the night froze them to pellets of stone.

5

ALMOST THIRTY YEARS earlier, Jo Carr had left the Devotionists and South America, where she had spent five and a half years as a teaching nun. The order had assigned her to a river valley between two remote ranges of the Andes. She quit before taking her final vows, but she had acquired a thorough knowledge of Spanish, which she spoke inelegantly, and a competency in various dialects of Quechua and Aymara. Back in the States, she had finished work on her master's degree in counseling.

For a while she had lived with a Buddhist graduate student in Austin, where she had a job at a Catholic college outside town. When that ended she went east, borrowed money from her moderately well-off parents and took the additional degrees the state required for a better job. A few years later, the college in Amesbury hired her. Now and then she had the feeling that some people at the college regarded her with caution. It was no secret that she had been a nun. She was resolutely secular in the counseling she dispensed.

In fact, it was impossible to suggest one road over another to kids who became virtually different people over the course of their college years. They might later bitterly regret something they had done or not done, a choice made that they came to believe they had been tricked into by a counselor covertly serving the wrong side.

Jo had been in trouble once. A number of years before, she had gotten to know a wealthy Catholic family whose daughter she had counseled at the college. Their daughter, who had become pregnant, ended by deciding to give her baby up for adoption to a pious Catholic family of means, so things seemed to have turned out well. The difficulty was that the recipient family came to regard Jo as a fellow Catholic who might provide more babies for friends in search of adoptive children. In the event, Jo found another student who wanted neither premature motherhood nor the sin, as she believed then, of abortion.

Jo brought the parties together. The fragile bark of human design being what it was, within a year things fell apart. Voyages of self-discovery found strange destinations; gathering storms broke. After something like a conversion experience — to what was unclear — it seemed the young birth mother wanted some relationship with her baby. Then she changed her mind. Discontents found their way up the college's chain of command and even Dean Spofford, the smoothest operator ever to package a denial of college liability in a letter of condolence, found the outcomes trying. However, the experience taught Jo to be extra-scrupulous regarding matters sectarian, and she kept her job.

In the course of resolving that incident, Jo had gotten to know some of the people at the Newman Club and a look-in at what had been a subculture within the Catholic Church. Jo Carr, who would long keep her sentimental regard for religion, had found it hard to dislike the Newman people. In the days before the Catholics got so aggressive in their anti-abortion politics, before the sexual abuse scandal among parish priests, the Newman clubbers were quite lovable, with their Masses said by young priests from Kerala or Swaziland. Some Catholic kids went to the Newman Center in their freshman year and soon drifted away. At Whelan Hospital Jo had seen one she remembered, a pious post–parochial schoolgirl named Maud Stack, who had produced the club's newsletter. Now Maud was a campus star, a *Gazette* editor whose idea of a club had nothing to do with dead cardinals. According to rumor, Maud had a romance going with one of her professors. Jo was not sure who the man was but suspected Steven Brookman, a witty man she knew slightly.

Whatever difficulties might presently befall the college or its students were unlikely to shock Jo Carr. In South America, at close quarters, she had seen a struggle toward mutual extermination so savage, fueled by such violent hatred between races and classes, that the very phrase "civil war" seemed an ironic euphemism. At the college she did what she could. A mind, as some brain-dead politician had once misquoted a fundraising slogan, was a terrible thing to lose.

Almost every year a kid was referred to the counseling office in whom Jo could detect the first signs of adolescent-onset schizophrenia. She was not qualified to work with its victims — there was a clinical psychologist at the center — but she knew the signs well enough. The too-wide smile, undercut by fear and wonder in the eyes, the futile attempted escapes into non sequitur, all the small signs of demeanor that signaled the beginning of the adventure. The descent of the innocent into half light, half life.

Far better, and one hoped less futile, was to talk to the merely troubled, beset by circumstance. Jo Carr's clients were mostly young women. Often their problem was some degree of culture shock or homesickness, things that could be dealt with by providing someone to talk to. Other kids had drinking problems, and a surprising number — surprising to Jo, and increasing as far as she could tell — had drug addictions. At times, and in the cases of students who placed a lot of trust in the college as an institution, the problem was pregnancy. The questions these girls had were almost always similar, and Jo's answers were too. There was no way around it, she thought. She hoped her answers were useful.

A sample question: "Should I tell my parents?"

Jo's answer would be: "You'll eventually feel you have to. That usually works out best in the end. If you're not a minor, you're not legally bound to get their permission to terminate in a state where abortion itself is legal. Get medical advice from someone you feel you can trust in a state where it's legal. It's legal here, for example."

There was more to it, which she generally omitted from the record. The unrecorded section, in substance, went like this: "Young students at this college are unlikely to be bounced off the household walls for getting pregnant — though life is full of surprises. Tell your mother first, let her break it to Dad. Dad, even if he's some foursquare right-to-lifing politician, is very likely to help pluck the mote from the apple of his eye. If your parents live separately, if you feel deeply apart from them, if they really aren't rational people, use your judgment. Consider that if you are not ready and have no resources, the result of bringing a pregnancy to term can bring down on you and on your child more suffering, poverty and unhappiness than you can imagine. If you terminate your pregnancy, you may also feel very guilty and deprived."

Adoption-wise, moreover: "Keep in mind that this is a college where students like you have been known to sell their fertilized eggs to eugenics-minded strivers. When it comes to facing an anxious, six-foot-one-inch, sculpted, preternaturally intelligent, Anglo angel of a basketball goddess, parents can be readily recruited for your love child. And often — not always — the young dad is an infant phenomenon himself. Keep it in mind.

"This may be the most important decision you ever, ever make," she would tell them. "Try very hard to get it right."

Every time, she was tempted to say, against her own good

sense and reason, "Pray for guidance." Of course she never did. She avoided, out of discretion and principle, any suggestion of religion, regardless of the kids' backgrounds. Any French movie critic, she believed, could bring more influential historicist doctrine to bear on his specialty than she could on advice to troubled youths. Sometimes Jo cried over the kids and their problems. But it was in Texas she did most of her crying. For a while there Jo had subbed as a teacher in a ghetto high school and had got to know a few of the kids. Girls she had counseled there would sometimes fall in love with their books, their curricula, with the process of learning itself, only to have it end for them with pregnancy. Then they would find themselves approaching baby-mamahood unassisted.

At the college, she had learned how to avoid sectarian problems. She had come to despise both the Catholic Church and its archenemies. As for causes unto death, in the montaña she had seen all the passionate intensity she could possibly endure and stay sane.

The conferences usually ended the same way. "Please stay in touch," Jo would say.

She was in her mid-fifties but looked younger. In dress she tended to fashionable dark suits, short- and tight-skirted in the turn-of-the-twenty-first-century style. Her salary was not so bad, better than that of some adjuncts.

There had been no appointments that miserable day, an icy gray morning that left windshields frosted and sidewalks treacherous. After her morning at the counseling center Jo worked the afternoon shift at Whelan Hospital. Whelan was the one connected with the college and performed abortions, prescribed birth control and often drew pro-life demonstrators.

As she started up the hill toward the hospital the sun broke through. In very little time students were on the college hill in T-shirts, tossing Frisbees. Then the sky turned misty and pale. A warm wind came up the valley. All at once the disorderly day prepared to present as spring. It was the kind of day salted with memories for Jo Carr. Maybe, she thought, for students too, because students arrived lately with recollections so much more complicated and brutal than the old ones.

Jo was just old enough to remember when places like the college played at being the world. Its students went out to rule their cloudy imperium and around the campus no one even locked a door. In days of old the college had presumed to send forth its light, a few homilies, to doomed praying Indians. In its own heart it never knew, and never learned, light or darkness — about either, or how to distinguish one from another. It sent out bookish young men, and eventually women, to save the world by generations. But the college had never really known darkness until they threw away the keys, and the shadows the place had pondered and reported and tried to witch away turned up at its doors.

As a volunteer at the hospital, Jo functioned as a counselor–social worker. Even there she sometimes felt uneasy, a necessity to keep her job, and her dialogue with patients was, by unspoken understanding, scrupulously secular. It was hard for Jo to be secular about pain, however. Might as well call it God's will as anything else, a process that was futile to interrogate. It was so much less of a burden not to attempt a ministration. How should I know why you got that awful stuff? Offer up your sufferings to the Holy Spirit if that gets you through the night. God takes pride in his providence. People felt better. So all of it gave urgent evidence of something. But what?

An odd thing had happened to Jo only weeks before. She had gone to visit a seven-year-old girl with a fatal, painful cancer. Her mother and father were there. The man was a swamp Yankee kind of guy. He wore a black jacket that might have been provided by a township to go with a job at the dump. He was not young. The mother was narrow-faced, pointy-nosed, small and whipped. The girl you could hardly look at without breaking down, so pale and helpless that it gave resonance to the term "life support." Suddenly the child's mother took the notion that her dying daughter should be baptized. In her surprise and confusion Jo thought in a rather panic-stricken way about priests, ministers, any clergy who might be on duty. All at once she heard herself saying, "I can do that."

This was true according to canon law when there was no time for delay. And maybe there was a defiance in it for her — the male authority and so on. So with water from the bright steel black-and-white thermos jug beside the bed and the medical machinery, she did it. She poured the ice water over her hand and tried to hold it a second, warm it just a little. Three cups of the hand invisibly sheeted with ice shards, a viaticum, Father,

Son, Spirit. And then the girl's mother wanted the same, and Jo did it. To the child's father, Jo said, "Sir?"

It was absolutely not her business. It was a presuming intrusion, patronizing, diminishing. She thought he was feeling that as strongly as she was. He also knew, as did she, that he would not hold it together, that the sacrament would lay him down and out and break him in half. Which made it even more intrusive, and so she properly went away. Yet when she did, her heart was soaring. Any good at all, she thought. The hope of it even. Even the slim fancied appearance of an invisible notion was better than nothing, suggested some significance for naked pain. On the college shuttle bus back to her office she felt guilty and cried.

At the top of the hill, a block or two from the hospital, four young Andeans were playing bamboo flutes. Jo had been vaguely aware of them for a few days and was used to the stratospheric pitch and spectral tunes, and to hearing them played around the campus. Three boys and a girl were busking there. Two of the boys wore tweed caps like old-fashioned British shepherds. The girl and the third boy wore beat-up fedoras. At their feet was a woven basket of the sort that was used all over the Americas for carrying fruit. These youths were not in costume — they were the real thing — Indians of the montaña. Watching them, Jo could almost place their valley, tucked into some high borderland, alternating the tropical and the alpine, speaking a language that was almost exclusive to that valley. All at once Jo realized that she could recognize the song they were playing. It was called "Sora," a song all children knew and could sing in several versions. She did not know the meaning of the words, only that the song somehow concerned the Milky Way, which in some of the mountain languages was known as the Sea of Fat.

Students had stopped to watch and listen, and a few took places among the Andean players. The music of the flutes was as hypnotic as it always had been. One flute, she noticed, was made of plastic instead of bamboo.

Jo could vividly remember an occasion from her days in the mountains, children on the edge of a village where she was staying, singing "Sora" with voices as innocent and clear as fresh rain sounding in the broadleaf palms along the dry-season forest trails. After the children's song the villagers were addressed by two men, an elderly white professor from the nearest provincial college and a local schoolteacher who spoke in the villagers' language.

What that experience had aroused in Jo Carr, then a young nun thousands of miles and so many years away, was fear and rage. Fear first, because she had mastered the local trails and her motorbike well enough to understand what was going on in the valley around her. The rage nourished itself afterward. In the montaña that evening she had assumed, as a listener, an expression of benign approval. People were watching her and she was very afraid. The people in the village crowd, she knew, were also afraid. It occurred to her now, standing on the manicured hillside of the college, that she was assuming the same complacent expression.

When the children had finished singing "Sora," the speakers explained the situation, the big picture. The collectives the government had established on confiscated estancias were a cheat and a lie. The people must know this. When things had been explained to them, the judgment of the people was never wrong. No one could arrogantly pretend to be above or outside it. And only those whom history had summoned to leadership could interpret the people's judgment. Why? Because only they understood history completely.

Nor could that judgment be appealed, based as it was on absolute mathematics and philosophy. The knowledge commanded by the leaders' chief was the opposite of lies. It was like the lines across the stars. They had been known to the people who had built pyramids all over the world. The lines led from a point near the Sea of Fat into the deepest desert, measured to a degree more correct than anyone on earth could perceive. Liars pretended knowledge.

The night birds had begun their trills and flutings. Night came suddenly at that latitude. The week before in a nearby village a number of people, peasants and local grocers whom the leaders called "the rich," had been boiled alive in rubbing alcohol after witnessing their children being eviscerated. They were accused of being spies for the auxiliary police, a charge that no one in the village really believed. After the killings, the army of the people had taken as much money as they could find and distributed it to the deserving poor.

"We are Robin Hood," shouted one of the people's soldiers, who in his bourgeois life had gone often to the cinema. He would subsequently be denounced over his previous indulgences and murdered with what was, then, still unbelievable cruelty. "Look at the pictures of the rich on the money," cried another. At a meeting at the edge of the village the people cheered, screamed actually, a sound that, like "Sora" and the speeches, Jo would remember for the rest of her life.

So there she stood on the hillside listening to the flutes and pretending to enjoy the concert, all over again.

Her experience in the valley had left Jo with variations on a recurring dream. Its setting was always the same, cobbled together out of recollections of the montaña and its valleys. Its contours were probably made partly from memories of what different local leaders of the movement had claimed life would be like after the only historically correct revolution in history. The dream was also composed of random images from the montaña, the villages, the Struggle, the visions of promise that the movement's leaders laid out for the imaginations of its supporters, and of her own early denial and finally nameless dread.

In the dream it is early evening, showing a quarter moon. The sky is far away. "So blue" was her dreaming thought. The clouds are transparent. Smoke from a dung fire rises to a point, the height at which the wind disperses it. The Four sound their flutes around a fire the color of the sky. "Sora." She never learned the words. So sweet but their meaning is unspeakable. The breath of the fluting marks the four directions of the winds. On high is Sirius and the stars near it in Canis Major where the Sacred Lines meet. Also the stars of Pictor, called by Western astronomers the Easel.

Canis Major was on the banner of the Struggle. The Spanish priests had believed that secret human sacrifices were made to Sirius and other stars. Surely they — practitioners of auto-da-fé — had also believed that the spectacle of ceremonial homicide was edifying. Everyone in Jo's dream is smiling at the sky.

In an empty space where some malefactor's house had stood there are panels of light blue plastic around a square of the exquisite sky. It is a window with no house. A sign under it reads: SORA. Maybe it meant freedom, or perhaps Sirius. I could sing it in my sleep if I knew the words, Jo always thinks before waking up.

Shivering beside the science building, she stood among the student audience. In the cooling early winter dusk, the young people smiled and applauded. Jo stayed with them, listening until some of the students wandered off and the musicians stopped playing. She was still standing on the hill when a colder wind settled in the valley and the college students began to drift off. One of the musicians, a light-skinned, delicately featured young woman, was taking contributions from the audience in her large broad-brimmed hat, embroidered on the crown with what looked like morning glory vines. There were many bills forthcoming. Finally the young woman looked Jo in the eye, tensing with a small smile.

She reminded Jo of someone she had once known. A pale man, eyes black as blood at night. Jo put the thought of him out of her mind.

She gripped her own shoulders to keep from trembling. She remembered the excuses the well-educated people, native and foreign, had made for the movement. All of them she had tried to believe when belief had come more easily. The effort of belief, the replacement of it with sheer terror and a sense of what she thought of as her own cowardice, had cost her. One price she had paid was the almost nightly reliving of awakening to find abomination in the stars. Her favorite stars too, the brightest and most beautiful she had ever seen. Spying out the heart of evil in the sacred lines of heaven made her suspect that perhaps the religious life was not for her. On the other hand, she thought, maybe it was.

6

A FEW DAYS LATER, Maud turned up at Brookman's office door and tapped her secret signal. She had an envelope with some kind of printout inside. "You have to read this. I need your reaction."

"I haven't time now, love."

He thought her look was suspicious. "Why?"

"I have a meeting," he told her falsely. He was anxious for news of Ellie.

She stamped her foot a little. She looked genuinely pleading. Childlike.

"Really," Brookman said, "I have to hurry . . ."

She handed it to him with what appeared to be a blend of anxiety and self-satisfaction. "Call me, Steve," she said. "Tell me what you think."

When she was gone, he locked up and went home without a thought of the envelope. She was always insisting he preview her writings.

In the Brookman house on Felicity Street — the larger half of what had been the marble-fronted Federal-style home of a single family — Steve Brookman prepared to grade and comment on his student essays. He was not particularly a drinking man but on this afternoon he poured a half snifter of Courvoisier, an expensive concession to his own self-pity.

Smart kids were wonderful if they could keep it all together, he was thinking, if nothing bad happened, though every year, somewhere in the college, something did. Whereupon Dean Spofford would call the parents, and you had to give it to the guy who had to do that. There were always casualties, of drugs or madness in general.

He was thinking of Maud and how utterly demure and innocent she appeared. These terms reflected the attitudes of his generation and she would probably be insulted by them. The young, young texture of her skin always astonished him. He was also wondering how he might be able to break things off with her, in spite of the fact that she was his advisee and had given up a junior year abroad for him. It was late in the semester. They were working on her undergraduate thesis.

Beyond anxiety, he was aware of feeling a kind of reckless, mindless joy.

Brookman had no native talent for intrigue. He had been careless and forgetful all his life. In twenty years of teaching he had never slept with a student before. College kids flirted, boys as well as girls. How could they not — the students had been the apples of their elders' eyes from preschool. During what happened to be Brookman's first semester with Maud, without intending any personal reference, a younger colleague of his had observed that innocent coquetry now led to innocent fucking. There was also innocent frenzy, innocent passion, the innocent, impalpable knife through the heart. Brookman was the one more experienced with consequences, and to that degree he had thought he could take care of her. Innocent love was not possible, love the least innocent of all things. For a long time he had believed he knew as much as anyone about love but that it had no nameable qualities.

He drank more than he ought have done if he intended to drive. He'd accepted an invitation to a party that evening, given by the college's famous resident artist. She was not truly in residence; she commuted by plane from New York but maintained a rustic roost with a Franklin stove and a picture window up in the hills for use on teaching days. A never-to-be-seen friend would fly her from Long Island in a vintage DC-3, the kind of plane in which Ingrid Bergman and Paul Henreid escape from Casablanca. It didn't get any hipper than that.

The artist, a tall woman in her fifties, affected a brunette style and black dress that suited her slim figure and large, expressive brown eyes. Brookman liked her work, which had Piero della Francesca–shaped women who were confined in some way — up against walls or prison bars, sometimes dead, sometimes portrayed as mounted condottieri in period breeches, cuirasses and greaves. The paintings invited narrative speculation from the viewer. There were some portraits too, of both men and women. Some of these pictures were in the college museum, which had given her a show. None of her work hung in her rustic hilltop house, however; there it was all West African art — masks, bronzes, elaborately worked cloth-and-feather fetish compositions, baskets, a lightning snake. These objects had been set up in dramatic ways in every public room in the house.

There were maybe thirty people at the party, most of whom he'd seen around the college. Two of the people he knew pretty well but rarely saw, a young female philosophy professor who had a history with Brookman and was present with her husband, and a frail, long-haired history professor named Carswell, who'd been working on his third volume of the origins, flourishing and destruction of Carthage. Carswell went to Tunis every year, and his first book was highly praised in the *New York Review*. His second volume was trashed by a rival and not noticed by supporters. He was still going to Tunis but looked a bit discouraged; years were passing without volume three. He told people he was rewriting too much. Behind his back, people were calling him Mr. Casaubon.

Brookman wished him well; he felt he had been in the same situation. He had a few drinks without paying attention to how many and went over to the historian.

"Hey, Dan, I ever tell you how much I liked your first book?"

It was true that Brookman had read and enjoyed the first volume on Carthage. But that had been pretty much enough Carthage for him.

"Yes, you did, and I'm grateful."

"I really liked it."

"Actually, the first volume on Carthage wasn't my first book."

"I didn't know that."

"No," said Carswell, "I realize that. I hope you'll like the next. Maybe I should say I hope you'll actually read it."

"Hey, I'm waiting." He put his hand on Carswell's shoulder, which was lower than his own. "But don't give yourself a hernia."

He had not meant to say that. It had come out wrong. He had meant to compliment and encourage. He looked back at Carswell, who was staring into his own drink. Best not to apologize. Anyway, Carswell had been insufferable. Brookman thought it was time for him to be going. He took one more round of the African art and found his hostess, the painter, at the door.

"This is the greatest collection of African art I've ever seen," he told her.

"Then you haven't seen many," she said.

Brookman looked at the woman in surprise.

"Buy it over there?" he asked her.

"Of course."

"Did you buy any slaves?"

No, no, he thought, driving home. Not what he had intended to say at all. There was some bitter herb under his tongue that night. Had there not been a contemptible figure in the days of Emily Post called The Guest Who Is Never Invited Again?

"Not that I give a shit," he said to the dashboard.

But his wife liked parties. Ellie liked people and people

loved her, and it would not do for him to lurch from house to house poisoning their social life in a fairly small place. He had no desire to establish himself as the inevitable asshole spouse. As for the people they socialized with — sometimes he enjoyed them, sometimes not. But Ellie had to have her pleasures until she went back to teaching again.

Ellie's popularity at the college, among both her colleagues and her students, was a source of great satisfaction to Brookman. He himself was not disliked. In fact he was widely admired, but not, like his wife, so affectionately regarded. He had been raised in a state orphanage in Nebraska, and his colorfully rendered recountings of early deprivations made him an exciting figure to the college's students. His courses were always oversubscribed, and one he had given, on his own *Smithsonian* article about a sunken Spanish Manila galleon, illustrated with his underwater photography, had got him a regular forty-five-minute program on PBS. He had been bitterly disappointed at its cancellation after one season, though not everyone in the English and composition department had shared his distress. In any case, it helped secure him a tenured position very early on.

His popularity and attractiveness led some to suspect him of womanizing, of conducting affairs with colleagues, wives and students. The suspicions were exaggerated. He had indeed dallied with faculty wives, but Maud, with whom he had quite fallen in love, was his first and only student lover and in that regard a violation of his principles.

After the party he sat in his college-owned house, in the

room he had chosen as an office — the room where the previous occupants had left their *National Geographic*s — and listened to Chet Baker's "Let's Get Lost."

His answering machine was on for calls from Ellie. There were fretful calls from Maud. Playing the messages back, he realized she had been drinking. Maud was not a cheap date; she had a hard head and could put a lot away for a girl her age. It seemed the wrong time to redefine a relationship. He failed to call her.

"Never apologize, never explain" was some vitalist supremo's line. Sound advice if anyone could hold to it. But within himself it was all he did. His conscience, or whatever it was, kept perfect time with him, stalked him adeptly. He would never be at peace with himself.

Maud's youth, unquietness, intelligence, passion and lack of judgment were irresistible to him. So shamelessly bold, reckless. They lured each other. She did it probably out of impatience for real life. He had no excuse but greed.

At college age Brookman was serving in the Marine Corps at a naval air station in the Mojave Desert. Immediately afterward he had worked in a cannery in Homer, Alaska, then as a crewman on a crab boat out of the same town. The pay was good, the work unbelievably hard for twentieth-century Americans. They had recruited farm boys from the Midwest who were ready to do it. The risk — most of what counted as serious accidents were fatal — was very high. A single night in the rack, with Arctic water sloshing around the berthing compartment, the pitch and toss, the port and starboard rolls, had felt to him like sure, sudden death. Brookman had panicked utterly. He had wanted not to die in cold water, not to breathe his last with his lips up against the overhead while the water rose over his head.

In his terror he went to sleep. It had happened to him before, in childhood — absolute fear succeeded by sleep. When he woke up in the rack he put on his gear, climbed up on deck into the sleet and went to work. The captain of the boat, an active member of the Alaska Independence Party, had a procedure for men demanding to quit once aboard, which was the impulse of every man jack who had never been at sea before. Quitters had to wait until an inbound boat was sighted. The captain would then sell them a drysuit. The price of the drysuit was deducted from the pay due them, and the price was high. They wore the drysuit to jump overboard into Norton Sound, and assuming they got pulled out successfully the rest of their pay — plus — went for the other skipper's trouble. For the genuinely ill, Brookman's captain might provide a breeches buoy. Appendicitis might eventually get you a Coast Guard helicopter. Brookman had other tough jobs, at sea and ashore, and he had done time in jail for no good reason.

The college's midnight music station was playing Chet Baker's version of "But Beautiful." As he poured himself a last drink, his wife's cat, Fafnir, came into his study and sat down on the sofa, a privilege he was not allowed when the mistress was at home. Fafnir looked at Brookman as though he'd like Chet Baker explained to him. Brookman leaned over and gently brushed him off. Fafnir seemed to like music but he was very stupid. He had to be brushed off things gently because he did not command cat-like grace and was capable of falling on his ear.

Fafnir licked his whiskers and promptly climbed back on the cushion, knowing Brookman lacked his wife's authority and persistence. Persian cats are dumb, Brookman thought, but some possessed mystical powers, and Fafnir was one of these. He could summon the presence of distant people from far places and reflect them in his vapid blue eyes. On this evening Brookman looked into Fafnir's eyes and saw there Ellie and his daughter, Sophia. Behind them, a snowfield stretched to the ends of the earth. In late summer the field would be gold with wheat, but now there was snow and also the biggest feedlot anywhere near White Lake, Saskatchewan. Ellie and Sophia were wearing little starched caps, looking like a couple of local Mennonites, which was essentially what they were. Sophia would be spending her days being instructed in her mother's faith, relearning the Gothic alphabet and reciting edifying verses in High German. There they dwelled in an eternal Sabbath.

Perceiving them in the occult cat's eyes, Brookman was suddenly overcome with terror. What if they're dead, the plane's wings icing, the pilots talking shop. What if Justice was on its way, striking as it will at the innocent and good? Chet Baker was singing "Moonlight in Vermont."

Brookman had met Ellie Bezeidenhout at his first teaching job, which was in Nebraska, where he came from. He had got the job after his Bhutan book was commissioned and completed. The position was at what could only be called a teachers' college, formerly a state normal school, which was now naturally called a university. Certainly not a normal, a term that opened vast caverns of misunderstanding. On one of his first days there he had picked up the course catalogue. The place may have been a normal, but as a university it was quite absurd. Its directory featured maniacally joyous photographs of faculty members beside their names and degrees that made them appear as a band of merry pranksters who did animal voices on a kids' cartoon show — *quack, baaa, oink.*

One faculty entry stopped him:

Professor of Anthropology Dr. Elsa Bezeidenhout, Ph.D.
B.S., Nazareth College, Saskatoon, SK
M.S., University of British Columbia, Vancouver, BC
Ph.D., University of California, Davis, CA

Elsa Bezeidenhout looked like a teenager. She was very blond, as — he later learned — was everyone in White Lake, SK. Her smile was wide but her face was long and her features were — how to say? — refined. He loved the "Bezeidenhout." They've been married eleven years and she is firmly Ellie Brookman now. "Why don't you use your maiden name?" he enjoys asking her. "So many women do."

"The students can't spell it," she says primly. "They can't even say it."

She knows she's being teased but won't react. On the rare occasions when he gets to hear her pronounce her maiden name, she utters a priceless interlacing of Plattdeutsch and Canadian vowels that only other people from White Lake could possibly understand. She's not crazy about the "Elsa" either. Chet Baker sang on.

Now it has to end with Maud. It's been a week since Ellie called to tell him she was pregnant. He tried to reason it. Maud, he thought, was there to grow up.

She's here to grow up. She has to learn a few things, and one of them is that everything comes to an end. Reasoning was not very supportive. Special pleas. As a friend of his had once claimed: "I'm not a womanizer. Just an easy lay."

She won't understand it now but eventually she will. It won't be easy. Also, it was always a good idea to break upsetting news — or say anything that engaged her emotionally — when she hadn't been drinking — which, after dark, was rarely. Maud was one of the great student juicers, a not uncommon group given the pressures of the college. The drink didn't seem to drain her energy or affect her grades. Such was the resiliency of youth. The semester was ending; they won't have to meet in class, and she will find herself another adviser.

Is this cynical? Yes, he realized it perfectly well. Still he felt compelled to reason a further defense. This is love, as it is sometimes called. It always has to end. In practice it has a morality all its own. Surely she didn't expect to marry him. In the unlikely event of such folly, she would walk in a year or two, chasing the smoke of the next fulfilling experience. Maud wanted fulfilling experiences. She wanted them for free. She's reckless, he thought — heedless, demanding, and she'll always be that way. She'll break a few hearts before she's through.

Chet Baker explained love, how it was funny, that it was sad.

7

PASSING HIS CLOSED WINDOWS on the street side of the quad the following afternoon, Brookman could hear his office phone ringing. Five or so minutes later, after he had opened the last lock that secured his office from the world, the phone was still sounding off. He let it ring as he hung up his coat. He had spoken with his wife from the Toronto airport minutes before, so there was no doubt in his mind that it was Maud. His cell phone was so frantic with messages from her, ranging from the apologetic to the drunkenly enraged, that he had been driven to turn it off. Whether Maud knew he was in the office or not, she was relentless. He let it ring. No signal or wire could convey what he had to tell her. In time she would show up at his office and he would say what needed saying. He threw the office curtains open because there were no longer any wonders to conceal.

The remnants of his fire simmered in the hearth. Every morning one of the college servants was dispatched to lay and start a moderate blaze in each of the offices. This would usually go out before the first appointments. Brookman tortured a flame from the kindling. The fire irons were folk art from a hospital craft shop in Rhode Island. They had an animal theme, horned and phallic. Over the mantel was a poster from the Museum of Modern Art depicting Picasso's *Boy Leading a Horse.* Brookman set the wicked poker in the andirons and seated himself on a handsome black leather sofa he had salvaged from the building's basement. He picked up the receiver. The silence on the wire was absolute. He imagined her palm pressed against the speaker.

Within minutes the phone began to ring again. This time, he thought, there might be news from Ellie on her journey, but the presence on the instrument, he was absolutely certain, was Maud. He heard street noises behind her. The Andean flutes. Traffic. When he replaced the receiver the phone rang once more.

The afflicted man was circling the quad outside. His hair was freshly and neatly trimmed to an old-time crewcut. He had newly rimmed glasses. Brookman had seen the man often enough that these refurbishings were regularly scheduled, seen to by whoever had chosen or been retained to assist his passage through middle age. He always appeared alone; Brookman had never seen him in company with anyone. Time passed, the telephone rang, and the afflicted man made his circuits.

Watching these grim winter circumambulations, breathing to the rhythms of his unrelenting phone, Brookman found himself thinking of an early summer day a few years before. It had been the last week of classes in the spring term. The mild sweet wind carried dogwood and azalea blossoms, mission fulfilled, message delivered. The college was busy with preparations for class reunions, graduations, hushed with the efforts of spring-struck adolescents striving against nature for diligence, getting ready for exam week. One of the professors in the English department was a tall, handsome, prematurely gray daughter of the coast of Maine named Margaret Kemp. Some said of Margaret that she burned with too bright a flame. At some point her comp lit class exploded into an explanation of the unitary systems behind the universe, galaxies beyond nebulae, counter-worlds intricately linked. Other instructors wore themselves out waiting for the use of their classrooms, colleagues stopped speaking to her, students mainly complained and fled. Not all.

When the college politely reclaimed its rooms, four students followed her outside. There, they sat down on the cold ground until after dark and Margaret continued to delve into the arcane systems beyond whose mere appearances the heart of the cosmos beat. One of the kids was a general's daughter. Two were the star horsewoman of the equestrian team and her boyfriend, a scholarship kid from Weed, California. The last was an unusually cultivated, impressive young man, a student from New Orleans.

Deep in the night, when the campus went quiet except for distant drunken yells, Margaret and her company of pilgrims were wandering the fragrant grounds, the four students trailing their cicerone like tourists at an antique tomb site. The campus police watched but did not question; professors had been weird for years. Morning came and another evening, and then the sun rose again on Margaret, hoarsely gesticulating, beautiful as life-in-death in her transfixion, and on the students, dead-eyed, weeping, laughing together, raising their hands in wonder at all that Margaret, once the smartest shipwright's daughter in Bath, had conjured out of the mornings and the evenings of a few days in May.

A woman from the counseling office named Jo Carr put a stop to it with an arm around Margaret, who seemed ready to slug her. The students wandered in circles. The psychiatrists treating them thought they were on drugs, which some of them may have been, but it made no difference. Two kids dropped out of school for a year, the two others for some months. The college accommodated them. Right after the exercise Margaret made her way to her house on Nantucket.

Margaret Kemp had a close friend at the college, another English professor with an office next to Brookman's, named Constance Haughy. Constance was an older woman who usually seemed quite sensible, but occasionally surprised. One night Brookman was working late when Constance's telephone began to ring next door. He concentrated on the piece he was finishing. Then, after two hours, he noticed something strange: the phone was still ringing and, he realized, had been ringing the whole time. When he left his office it was still ringing. Walking home, he knew that it must be Margaret attempting to reach

ROBERT STONE   69

out. The night-shift cleaners later swore the phone had gone on ringing all night. The next day, on Nantucket, Margaret hanged herself in her garage, kicking away her bicycle.

As usual, nothing was free. Margaret was far from the first faculty suicide. Historically, violent death was never too long away. Adolescent turbulence, middle-aged despair, alcohol. Not to mention heroin and coke and speed. The pressure of relentless competition generated toxins catalyzed by the disorientation, the separation from love, the random sex, the sheer cold uncaringness of the college. When these elements came together it could be quite unsettling in the cozy firelit libraries and among the dreaming Gothic spires. Which was not to say the place lacked its pleasures, large and small.

The papers Maud had given him the day before lay on the desk. He pushed them away, then opened the envelope and took them out. The piece proved to be an article she had written for the weekly *Gazette*. The text seemed to be an objection to the anti-abortionist demonstrators who picketed Whelan Hospital each week.

One page that hadn't come through clearly showed photographs of some animal or other. Brookman put it under the light to see more, but the shades blended into invisibility. The captions were unreadable too. On one of the following pages the pictures were similarly obscured, but the caption was plain: "Cute kiddie pictures courtesy of the right-to-life folks."

"Ever ask," the text read, "in the name of what authority

do they harass women who choose to exercise their rights as full human beings? Most of them are dispatched by the Holy Romantic Megachurch. We know the Holy Romantic Megachurch loves cute kids. It's in the papers every week; the priests of this religion can hardly get enough cute kids. If women decide to terminate pregnancies, how will the guys get their hands on enough institutionalized or semi-institutionalized adolescents to instruct? Think about it!"

This was the paper he had left unread, the one she had specifically asked him to read.

He read on.

"This intrepid band of intimidators treat us to their visits and their cunning fetus pictures about fifty-seven times a year. If they don't come in the name of the Holy Romantic Megachurch, they represent the Assemblies of God, assembled by God for the purpose . . ."

Of course there was more. Brookman put the page under the light to see the picture. He thought it might have been a person, a child.

"Holy shit," Brookman said aloud.

Of course it was the kind of thing she would do. I could have talked her out of it, he thought. If he had read it. If he had not been dodging her phone calls.

"You guys might not be able to tell, but these deformed children are made in the image and likeness of the Great Imaginary Paperweight in the Vast Eternal Blue. It's true that the Great Paperweight is also the Great Abortionist — a freeze-chilling twenty percent of the sparkly tykes he generates abort — but he don't like some girl doin' it.

"His eye is on the sparrow and he's got all his creatures covered, even those who aren't as cute as the wee life forms his assembled fusiliers carry. Remember, there's life after birth, as the Assembled Ones never tire of reminding us. That's what prisons and lethal injections are for. He's the Great Torturer, and he wants nothing more than to fry your ass eternally — not for just an hour, not for just a year, but always."

She had gone too far in writing it. She had gone too far with him. She would go too far all her life. As for him, there were boundaries to his foolishness and selfishness. He had gone briefly to prison for it once, otherwise he had always been lucky. He had loved her. Loved would be the word. Lover, older brother. Father almost — she confided in him, maybe said to him what she would have said to her father but dared not. In loco parentis, one might cynically say. Or not cynically say.

Maud's father was a widowed New York policeman from somewhere out in Queens and Maud was plainly crazy about him. At length she would mock and jeer this man, do impersonations of him, imitate his hard-edged accent, unaware that she sounded like him without trying. The idea of a policeman with a personality like Maud's was frightening. Is he a religious fanatic? Because Maud is, regardless of the side she's on. She had come to the college impacted in the sort of antique Catholicism Brookman thought had disappeared from literate circles a generation ago, thin-lipped and bitter, to every man his cross.

Now she dealt the same card reversed. Armed with the child-ish energy of a parochial school minx, reciting every dirty word that's ever occurred to her.

What she thought of instinctively as her moral derelic-tions were at once deliberate, heedless and passionate. She has described her own petty thievery to him in a state of fascinated self-laceration. She has told him that as a teenager she was "abnormally devout." Now this, which will probably go viral online. It will circulate online and be darkly cherished by the wrong audience.

She's a policeman's daughter, he thought; does she not know what's out there? Does she expect nothing but cheers from all directions? He was, after all, her faculty adviser; he might have talked her out of this folly, which would surely bring down on her more trouble than she knew. But of course he had com-menced to abandon her.

The telephone, he noticed, had stopped ringing. He went to the window and looked out at the quad. Her cell phone was off when he tried it, and no one answered the phone in her room. He wondered if he might hear the Morse tattoo against his door.

The *Gazette* was due out the next morning. It occurred to him that the other editors there might have the sense not to run it. But those editors were kids like her. Why would they feel they should restrain the general rage at the overreaching, cor-rupt harassment of the churches?

Then it came to him, outside reason, that she might have

effected some kind of curse on his marriage — his wife and the child she carried. Of course: the child unborn. At the same time, he thought, he could not leave Maud alone and friendless in that place, and he went out to find her.

It was getting cold again outside. Across the street from his quad gate in the Taylor Library someone had lit a fire in the Great Hall, a quasi-medieval concoction from the prime of Stanford White. It was beautiful beyond the sneers of modernists and postmodernists, beyond authenticity. The firelight glowed invitingly in the leaded windows. *Why this is hell*, Brookman thought. *Nor am I out of it.*

8

ON FRIDAY MORNING Maud woke up to sleety rain. Though she could hear his telephone voice in her head, she realized that he had never picked up. She had not reached Brookman, and she only partly remembered making her way back to the dorm room from a booth in one of the bars near the river. She thought they must have told her to leave. Shell was searching their closets when she saw that Maud had awakened. She picked up a fresh copy of the *Gazette* and laid it on Maud's bed.

"Hey, girlfriend," Shell said, "notoriety is driving you to drink. You were staggering last night."

"Shit," said Maud softly.

"Well, there's your story."

Maud stared blearily at the college paper. Her column was front page left, with the jump on page three.

She got painfully out of bed and drank from her warm bottle of water and dressed.

"They left the pictures out."

"Well, somebody looked the conditions up and put them

online. With your picture too. Like you may get some shit over this."

"Good."

"Me, I love it," Shell said, "but I ain't gonna be standing next to you in any pictures in case you get famous like Joan of Arc. I got semi-stalkers already. Like my lately old man who just got born again again."

Maud rose slowly and walked unsteadily toward the bath-room.

"Your beloved mentor was up here looking for you last night," Shell told her. "Like he came twice. A big old professor coming to the squalid chambers of us waifs. For you, his sweet-heart. Only he was on his way to the airport to pick up his wife, I guess, 'cause he got a call from her."

"Shut up!" Maud shouted and slammed the bathroom door.

When Maud came out, still pale, Shelby was contrite.

"I always talk too much in the morning, sweet thing. Bird-seed under my tongue."

Maud stood weeping. And in her tears she looked to Shell like a savage child Shell never before glimpsed in her friend.

"I don't know what to do."

Shell went over and hugged her.

"Maud, honey, I been there. I been so unhappy. I been so scared. This, by God, happens to us."

She left Maud in the middle of the room and went to look out the window. Bums lining up for the church feeding, like pigeons.

"It's all good," she said. "Except how it sucks. Listen, Maud, go home. That's what you do. Get out of this laughing academy. It's break next week; a few days won't hurt your line. Go home and get away from him and me and this *vida loca* up here." She took Maud's duffel bag out of the closet and put it on the bed. "Get out of town before—"

"I want to see him," Maud said. She had stopped crying. Her mouth tightened, her teeth clenched behind a thinning of her long lips. Her jaw trembled. She pressed her nails into her palms.

Shell shook her head.

"Uh-uh."

She emptied Maud's drawer into the bag and went to her own closet and filled the bag with various things—jackets, a beret, some bracelets.

"Hey, lookie, I'm gonna give you cool shit of mine I never paid for. My bling and my star-quality wardrobe and starlet shoplifting trophies. You can't have my dope or my gun, but."

She put her best fake-fur coat around Maud's shoulders and turned her roommate toward the door and hugged her again.

"Keep warm, Maudie-pig. I love you round the neck. Don't drink so much, your ears'll swell up. It's true!"

Maud went out but left her bag on the floor. Shell did not pursue her, only watched from the window as her friend headed up the street toward the college with the fake fur wrapped around her shoulders. Then Shell stared blankly at the sky and sighed.

It had come to Maud that Brookman, returned wife or not, had a class scheduled that morning. As she passed Bay's en route to the college, Herbert, the café's chief of inmates, defying the weather at his outside table, bellowed a hoarse greeting at her, demanded Shell, whom he so loved. She hurried on toward the quad, Shell's coat close around her, and began to run.

At the quad the locks slowed her. She failed to intercept Brookman coming out of class and so went to his office in Cortland Hall. She sounded no tattoo for him this time, just three knocks, each knock a little louder than the one before. He opened the door, showing no surprise.

"Come in, Maud."

"'Come into the garden, Maud, for the black bat, night, has flown.' That it?"

"Sit, sweetheart."

"You don't want to touch me? Don't you want to shake hands?"

He took hold of her hands.

"Better close the curtains, huh?" Maud suggested.

"I looked for you last night."

"But you had to go pick up your wife at the airport."

"Yes. Remember, I told you my wife was coming back."

"Did you? Yeah, I guess you did. That why you avoided me?"

"What I wanted was to catch you sober and in an orderly state of mind."

She pulled a hand free and, Brookman thought, came close to hitting him.

"I was concerned about you, Maud. How could I not be? And you know my wife was coming here. She's pregnant."

"Pregnant," Maud said, "really? That's ironic, isn't it? Timely topics."

"Maud, sit down."

She stood where she was. A disturbing notion occurred to Brookman. He felt he had been given an insight into what her father, the detective, might be like.

Brookman himself felt tired enough to sit down in his emblazoned captain's chair. *Lux in umbras procedet.*

"We never said in so many words that our lives were going to change," he said, "but we knew. Lives always change. You're old enough to know that now."

"No," she said. "Not me. I ain't."

"What drove you to carry on like that about abortion?"

"Whatsa matter," she asked, "you didn't like it?"

"It was all you, my young love. But it's likely to get you more trouble than you bargained for."

"Get you trouble? Get your *wife* trouble."

"Sit down, Maud. No, I don't mean that." He saw that she was wrapped in an absurd fake fur and she smelled of alcohol.

"I'm sorry you didn't like it. Why didn't you read it? Would you have told me not to publish it? Maybe you would've told me not to publish it."

"No. I might have had suggestions, I guess. I got worried."

"That why you came looking for me last night?"

"I wanted to be sure you were all right. Grounded. And that you had thought a little about reactions. You were out."

"And you had to pick up your wife."

"Hey, Maud, you knew about my wife. Did you expect me to leave her at the airport?"

Maud reacted to his flash of anger. She leaned against the back of the chair that faced his desk.

"Why didn't you read it, Stevie? For God's sake. I was showing off for you."

Brookman stood up.

"Maud. My Maud. I want to be your teacher. I want us to be something in each other's lives. We cannot be lovers now."

"I know what the answer is," she said. "You'll be my eternal teacher. I'll be your eternal student." She watched him from the corner of her eye, looking venomous and sly.

"There is no answer to these things."

"Oh yeah, there's an answer. We'll go to Paris. Want to take me to Paris?"

"You better sober up, kid."

"I'll become a nun like Jo Carr used to be and I'll get my father to cut your prick off and we'll live in France and write cool letters to inspire future generations of assholes. Like me and you, Prof."

"I'm a human being, Maud. Same as you. You're gonna see that someday."

"You see how you hurt me, Stevie?"

"Yes, Maud."

She felt dizzy and her mouth was too dry for any more questions or suggestions.

"I hurt you, Maud," he said. "But you . . . you knew that —"

"Don't say it," she said.

Then she went outside to the quad. He sat in his captain's chair and watched her walk away.

When Shell got back to their dorm room, the bag she had packed for Maud was gone, and Maud with it.

9

EDDIE STACK HAD developed an odd skill. He was able to comb his hair — what was left of it — without looking at his own face in the mirror. He kept his gaze above the hairline. Some foreign wit had observed that after forty a man was responsible for his own face. Stack was over forty; in fact he was just over sixty-five, and he desperately did not want any more responsibilities beyond those he bore.

The face wanted answering for. Young, he had never got enough of it. Don't think he hadn't looked in mirrors then. He had the deadpan, dumb mick face that could be transformed within a fractal to the deadliest of satirical grins. And the assumed angry face, the hassled face, the put-upon, uncontainable-rage face that would break his partners up in the middle of a collar. The false smiles and the semi-genuine smiles and the honest smiles that were not entirely unstudied. Not until he had gone into the job had he realized how attractive he was to women. Most women kind of loved all police officers, but Detective Stack was envied in his appeal. There was also, he vaguely knew, a mug of true rage, and that was one he never looked at and yet privately had worn sometimes. His entire life was private now and he knew he must wear it very often.

Look at the face on him, his mother used to say. Fondly. But the face on him now, the one he might have to avoid in the mirror and the one he wore on the street, was another matter. Richmond Hill was an immigrant neighborhood. Most people there now simply did not resemble him. They were not fair or tall. They were not bleeders, as white boxers had once been called in the fight game. When he wore his face on the street — a face now flayed by alcohol and high blood pressure and a volatile temperament — he could imagine he was being spotted as a boozy Irishman, a slave to drink and an aging ruffian. To what might be on Lefferts Boulevard a stare of curiosity at one of the aboriginal occupants of Queens by a recently arrived Bengali or Mauritanian or Parsee and those he suspected as despisers of his kind, he showed the watery blue eyes, the rosy face. His strategy was to take his glasses off so that he would not see clearly the expressions of passersby or his own reflection in store windows. Beyond his own front hedges, which he paid a friendly Ecuadorian to trim, he truly did feel responsible for his face. Almost, he thought, ashamed.

What caused him to have his bushes trimmed by a hired man was actually what drove him nearest to actual shame. He went on his errands step by step and only after using — or neglecting to use — his three maintaining inhalers. He had emphysema that the doctors now called severe. So outstripped on the sidewalk by people twenty years older than himself, blocking the progress of young women uttering impatient sighs behind him, he tried not to notice, or even to see straight. He felt ashamed of himself. Early on, before the diagnosis, he had stopped cold climbing the second flight of stairs at the deep-down Jackson Heights subway station. About to pass him on the way down was a beautiful young woman, one to speculate about, a babe. Dry-drowning as he was, she got his attention. "Oh sir!" she said. "Oh sir, can I help you?" He wondered if he would ever be the same after that.

Smoking had done it, as well as and especially his useless — as he saw it — presence at the twin towers. He never mentioned that, not that there was anyone to mention it to. Plenty of people he knew had been there. Some, quite a few, had died there. Then there were those who had been there a month and a half after and talked about nothing else. There were those who had not been there and said they had. What Stack knew was the dark side of it, by which he did not mean the misled lads from afar with their faith-based initiatives, or the poor victims, God help them, but a different human dimension. Nothing was so bad it didn't have a dark side, Stack thought.

On a warmish morning in December he set out for the boulevard, a quarter mile downhill. It was cloudy, without the stimulation of winter. He did not need the paper to know it was a bad-air day. His tactical plan was to walk the downhill stretch, past the tidy houses of his enterprising neighbors, and buy a *Times*. He had once been a follower of events, but it was pretty much the sports section now. Besides the *Times* he would buy a *Post,* because it was Friday and he wanted the Sunday line. Stack had been firmly ordered to walk on errands rather than drive, the principle of use it or lose it.

He walked down the boulevard with his practiced obliviousness to what he had grown up calling the candy store, where Morris had sold egg creams and reportedly run a handbook. It was owned by a Pakistani now, an old man in a white cap that showed he had made the hajj to Mecca. He had turned out to be a jolly old-timer, cheerful, even jokey, though not as hilarious as Morris had been. A glum young relative of the old man's was at the counter this day. Stack bought the papers and took the most level route home.

The house was neatly kept, although his household appliances needed replacing. The furniture was a museum of early-sixties style. Stack did not shop for furniture or appliances. He had bought maritime prints at one point, and they were on his walls, along with a painting Maud had done as a teenager. The prints and the painting cheered him somewhat. After his wife died and Maud passed her devout stage, he had removed the crucifix from the living room and carefully tucked it away beside Maud's tarot cards, which she had wrapped in silk. He took down all the religious sacramentals and put them in a closet, except for a reproduction of a Leonardo, *The Virgin and Child with Saint Anne.* That hung in the upstairs hall. He felt a little guilty about the stuff; it bothered him, religion aside.

He would not put the objects in the garbage, which would be grossly disrespectful, and he did not want to outrage the sanitation guys.

In the evening he took his second walk of the day, to an old Presbyterian church that now had a Korean congregation. The church basement was the location of his AA meeting. No Koreans attended. An Italian-American man in his mid-seventies — slightly demented, maybe a little wet-brained — stood at the coffeepot near the door, welcoming everyone who passed through with a "Tanks for comin.'"

Afterward Stack would not remember a great deal about this particular meeting. The usual people were there. A couple of guys doing probation, half of them loaded. A few earnest Christians, an old starker from the furriers' union of long ago. Black guys, white guys.

The speaker, a man who had been off the sauce for a year. He looked young. He was slick, he was a musician. This was his share: As a boy, he told the meeting, he and his family had observed Passover with a Seder. In accordance with tradition a glass of wine was set aside for Elijah.

"This was not sweet Concord stuff because my family did not go in for that kind of wine. This was Lafite Rothschild. So my party trick as a child was I would sneak out, grab a man's coat and a hat I could find somewhere. Then I'd hobble in doing an old-man shtick — the prophet himself. And I'd grab the wine and drink. This amused all my relatives.

"So," said the young man, "I've been in eternal pursuit of my childhood faith."

Stack laughed in sympathy, but a feeling of deep sadness overcame him. He did not stay for the Serenity Prayer. He had the loved daughter who was rash and rebellious. Whenever he needed or wanted his wife, she was dead. He had always had the strength, or at least the toughness, to resist self-pity.

A momentary lapse, he thought. That was the joke he made to other policemen when some impulsive perp had tried to pull off some mindless caper.

"The momentary lapse of a ne'er-do-well," he used to say, breaking everybody up.

"Tanks for comin'," said the guy as Stack went out. He took the easiest route home.

Climbing the porch steps — like the steps to the upper floor — exhausted him. He sat down in the nearest armchair to recover his breath. Immediately he knew that Maud was home, and the ways he knew propelled him back along their history, in a way that raised and battered his heart. There was the perfume, the marijuana, the booze smell that had not been loosed on the house since her last departure, and under these, in his weak moment, all the effluvia of her childhood beloved and terrifying, of joy and rage. He stood up unsteadily and, having a practical side, reached in his pocket for the inhaler.

The stairs were a hassle but he lived from day to day. There in Maud's bed was the lovely mess of her, hair over the pillow and the rain-wet clothes scattered around. The worst thing about her was the smell of tobacco, which, he decided, he would not abide. Not a word had come from her, but the Christmas holiday would soon be on them, something he paid little attention to but of course she would be home for that. She looked comfortable enough and would have been drinking whatever she'd brought, so he left her there.

10

IN THE LIVING ROOM he took up his reading, a book from the branch library — borrowed in its scant opening hours — on some of the intelligence aspects of the Second World War. Patton's Phantom Army. Choosing the beaches for Overlord. He read his book until he heard Maud come out of her room.

"Hi, kid," he said. "You didn't say you were coming. I didn't think you would."

He asked her how things were, how school was, as he had when she was in high school.

"It's all good," she said. "It's fun. It's interesting."

"Did you bring some poetry with you? Because I never read as much poetry as I should."

"No," she said. "Sorry." She stood for a moment with him and started up the stairs.

"Hey," he said, "I could take you out to dinner."

"No. I'm like invited."

"Another night while you're here?"

"That'd be good."

"I don't go out much," he told her. "I gotta save my energy. For serenity, you know. 'Cause you don't give me much."

Is he kidding? she thought. He wasn't, but he was hoping for a smile in return.

"Hey, Dad, is there anything to drink in here?"

"No," he said. "Sobriety in here."

He was lying about there being nothing to drink. He was keeping a bottle of Jameson, out of defiance of the devil as it were, not drinking it. This was dangerous work, but an admired friend of his had done it. Maud happened to know where it was.

"Mind if I smoke a joint before I go?"

He didn't answer for a while. He had put up with her marijuana before. He had smoked it in the job. Coke, too, sometimes.

"You know," he said, "that crap is blood on your hands. Just like cocaine these days. A lot of poor people in Mexico get killed over that."

He sighed and told her to smoke it upstairs. When she was upstairs she made her sneaky way to the attic, to where her father's self-challenging liquor was. The bottle was in its box, untouched. He never went up there and she could replace it the next day. On the way to her own room she passed what had been her mother's small office, pretty much unchanged since her death almost four years before. Inside was a bulletin board on which her parents had tacked up her drawings and various printed writings, articles clipped from school papers and poems she had decorated with colored inks.

Under the board sat an ancient computer that Maud had updated so her mother could go online. The print on the screen could be enlarged. Dad had propped her mother's picture on the machine and Maud, clutching her stolen bottle, tried not to look at it. Still, she had paused too long not to hear the house of her childhood. His wise-guy voice; Mom, her story voice and laughter. The TV, her own footsteps on the stairs, her parents and her own kiddie ghost.

To get over all that she had to weepily light up her weed and break her nails on the whiskey cap and drink it raw. Poor guy, the hero he was finally trying to be. Because whoever the hero cops were, her dad had not been one of them. She felt terrible about the bottle. The weed was excellent. Dumbing-down weed. No one in this place but me, and I'm not here. She put the dope away and hid the bottle.

"You look nice," he said when she was going out.

"Really?"

He looked depressed. She laughed at him. She could not stand his company for another half minute. If she could laugh at him, she thought, she could laugh at fucking Brookman.

"Have fun," her father said.

11

"HOW DID YOU WASH dishes up there?" Brookman asked his daughter. "In the river? With your hair?"

He was helping Sophia wash dishes while Ellie worked in her office, catching up on the mail. Sophia sang Mennonite hymns as she worked.

"The river was frozen, Daddy. I mean, that's so silly." She seemed at least as disapproving of the silliness as amused by it. It took her a second to laugh. "With my hair?"

She's a pocket-size Bezeidenhout, Brookman thought. He thought of saying it to her, but he did not want to render her too perplexed in the process of cultural reentry. The twice-a-year trips between White Lake and Amesbury entailed a passage between the recitation-readings of biblical verses in High-German Gothic script and the latest e-mail abbreviations, and required a measured transition. On occasion Brookman had tried to find out how she was handling it and asked her. He was told the experience was variously cool, very fun and weird, but not really.

"More weird up there or down here?" Brookman asked her that night when they had finished the dishes. He had been to the place twice, long ago. He considered himself well traveled but it was very difficult to feel at home in White Lake. "The last time I was there it felt like there were people assigned to be nice to me. Like two people. Everybody else pretended I wasn't there. It was before you were born, Sofe."

"That's how the people are," Sophia said. "They've known me since I was little, though." She thought about it for a minute. "If they don't know you, they don't know what to say. So they don't say anything. And you don't. And pretty soon it's like you aren't there. And then they act like you aren't there. And then you sort of aren't there."

"I've felt like that in a few places, Sofe. Not only in White Lake."

"Like they don't always recognize me in my American clothes. I say like Hi in *Muttersprache,* and they go, Sophia! The kids. They call other people 'the English.' They call Americans 'the English.' They call other Canadians 'the English.' They call all outsiders 'the English,' even if they're French."

Ellie was coming down the stairs.

"It's an unusual community, you know," she said. "There are very sophisticated people in the Old Synod, you'd be surprised. Very wheeler-dealer some of them."

"Yes indeed," Brookman said.

"Daddy's asking which is weirder coming to. White Lake or here."

"Oh, ya? So which?" Ellie asked. "As a personal experience?" Before Sophia could answer, Ellie interrupted her. "Of course Sofe is a star exotic in both places, remember," she said to Brookman. "So her experience is conditioned by that."

"They're both weird," Sophia said. "I wouldn't want to be there all the time. I'd miss too much. Except sometimes I think I would. Be there."

"When you want to be a little girl again you do," Brookman said.

Sophia left the room quickly.

"I made her cry," Brookman said.

"It's a tough transition." Ellie leaned on the sink and smiled at the clean dishes. "Shit, Stevie, you made me cry too."

"I'm so happy," he told her. He was very glad about her being pregnant, but he did not really feel happy at that moment. He was glad to veer away slightly from what he knew most made her cry.

"It's emotionally tiring," Ellie said. "The trip itself, the wind, the overheated airports and customs. Do you know U.S. customs took an orange from Sofe once? I said to them, 'Where the heck do you think the orange is from, Baffin Bay?'"

"They wouldn't know where that was," Brookman said.

"Ya got that right, eh."

"The Canadian customs guys, when they're bad, they're worse. The Americans act like zombies. Your guys think they're cute. Comedians. They're hostile and sarcastic. They do Scotch standup comedy. Boreal wit."

They stood in silence for a while by the sink. Brookman watched his wife, and though she had spoken of tears she was dry-eyed. He prepared himself for the inevitable. But it did not yet come.

"Once," Ellie told him, "Sofe and I were in the meetinghouse up there just after worship, and we're having the chat you two were just having—you know—the difference, up there, down here, blah blah. Which is weirder? Here or the Community."

"We've given her a life lived in deviation," Brookman said.

"At least," Ellie said, "we've given her that!"

Brookman strongly agreed.

"Maybe because it's after worship, Sofe asked me, Does Daddy ever pray?"

"What did you tell her?"

"She was small, maybe five or six. I said, Oh ya, ya, he prays the way 'the English' do sometimes. Untrue of course."

"I don't know if it's untrue." He folded his arms and walked away from the sink to the kitchen window. "I find the kind of prayer you—I mean your once people—do . . . uncongenial."

"I'm sure, Stevie."

"Look," he said, turning to his wife a bit drunkenly. "What's the use of it? You can't ask God for anything. You can't request special treatment. You can't pray for an intention."

"No deals," she said. "Big God, little you. Sofe can tell you herself. Do you think she thinks of herself the way an American child would?" They both looked around to see if she was listening and lowered their voices. "She'll tell you how we pray. How we used to pray."

"She . . . ," Brookman began, but Ellie interrupted him.

"You worship Almighty God. You thank Him for his glory and you worship his will. He sent his Son. What must be, must be. You find his will and glorify it. You trust and live rightly and love. No deals."

"You shame me," Brookman said.

"Good," she said. "I love you. I'm sent to explain to you that you're other than the hot shit that you and others think you are. With the self-pity and indulgence the yokels in White Lake would call pride."

"Pride," he repeated dully.

"I'll tell you something else," Ellie said. "In my childish superstition I too still believe that God wills what I must do." He watched her put a hand to her mouth, stunned almost at her own words. Thrilled and frightened at what he thought she might say. She let him lead her out to the cold rainy porch that opened to a dying acacia and the wooden top of a defunct well. They had tried for such a long time to have a second child. They laughed about her country potions. His wearing boxer shorts for a year, on the advice of some friend of Ellie's. But they had never said a word about praying.

"But we did it, Ellie. We did it. Shouldn't it be a sign for us? Isn't it a blessing?"

"After so long," she said. "So much trying."

She turned her face away.

"I'm only who I am, dear one. Is it a blessing? If I let your pride dishonor me and my . . . children, I will have to feel my way. I will have to feel his pleasure, and if you do dishonor me — and in my benighted state I think you dishonor Him through me — I don't know what will be commanded. I'm sorry, my Stevie, my love.

"This will sound stupid. I love you next to God. Don't think I'm over the top. We're not in an opera. You see that's a commonplace, eh. All the girls where I come from, it's required. Commanded. You're my husband. You're my Stevie too. But I have to feel that's really how it goes. That has to be how it goes from now on. I must feel the rightness of things, the pleasure of things. You must make me have that."

He moved a little apart from her, still holding her hand.

"I don't think you ever put it to me that way before," Brookman said.

"No, I suppose. It would have been pretty fucking uncool, back in the day. Right? But you knew, didn't you?"

"Yes."

"And the old stuff comes back. We're getting old. Maybe just me. Old stuff comes back, maybe just when I go up there."

"Is the old stuff all we have?"

"It's all I have, Stevie my darling. Of course I'm not as smart as you."

12

MAUD ENDED UP in some mobbed-up club in the Meat-packing, thin film of blow on the bar, practically, more of it on the ladies' room fixtures. The guy said he was on Wall Street. Well, his brokerage house was in Jersey but he lived downtown. Not far from Ground Zero.

"Really, my father was at Ground Zero for about half a minute." She let that go. "My old man don't work, he's a cop in Queens." The place she woke up in was a filthy apartment that smelled of asbestos and lead and dead people and guys making free telephone calls to Poland. He was gone but she didn't steal anymore or fuck up assholes' apartments for revenge. She might have done it once. She tried drinking his bargain scotch and could barely keep it down. The guy had left a condom floating in the toilet, which was kind of reassuring in its disgusting way. No shower, just a crummy bathtub with feet. That at least, she thought. It was a sort of date rape, but she thought the hell with it. She wasn't sure but he hadn't seemed to get it on. Maybe, she thought, he put the condom in the john to impress her. To induce happy false memories. Anyway, she got out of there, went home and cleaned up properly.

She slept again, but when she woke up her thoughts were about Brookman and she could not bring them to order. She tried to bring Brookman's wife into the focus of her memory. It was ridiculous, so ridiculous — the Brookmans — that in the midst of her pain and distraction, she had a vision of the absurdity of her own grief and loss.

Female students often discreetly observed Brookman's wife. Smiley face, big teeth, whitey blond hair in a ponytail, you could hardly tell if she was getting gray. Her eyes were a little close together and wild blue. She wore big horn-rimmed glasses. Some of them called her a dog. But with big tits. She had a big ass, oh yeah, some said her ass was humongous. But that was only because she had one and some of them didn't. Her neck was wrinkly, her face too, from the sun. She dressed badly. She looked like one of the women on the PBS nature shorts you saw when you were a kid. Oh, Maud thought, there were a million happy-go-lucky women wearing khaki shirts being smart in nature shorts and sticking their fingers in wombats' ears but there was only one Brookman. And only one me. Maybe on the next canoe trip she can wander into quicksand and they'll find her horn-rims on the top and the rest of her thirty million years later. Laughing and crying, she spun around in her smoke-filled room until she sank to her knees by the bed, pressing her face into her forearm.

She burst out of her room to look downstairs and saw her

father reading the day's mail with a copy of the *Gazette* beside him. He looked up at her gravely.

"I owe you a bottle of whiskey," she said. And she wanted to say don't look so pathetic, and there were so many other things she wanted to say.

"Forget it," he said coldly.

"No, I'll get you one right now. I'll go out. I'm really sorry. I've been out of my head."

"Yeah. So forget it."

She breezed past his chair to get a glass of cold milk. He followed her into the kitchen.

"Hey, Maud," he said. He held up the college paper. "What's this?"

"That's my contribution to the *Gazette,* Dad."

"Don't they have a thing called hate speech?"

"It is not hate speech," she shouted at him. "It's the advocacy of the rights of women to access and control their own lives. And not have them controlled by — you know who I mean, don't you, Dad? Controlled by hypocrites. You were the one who told me Grandpa's stories of Fat Frank Spellman in New York."

"Never mind Fat Frank Spellman," Stack said. He ran out of breath and sat down next to his oxygen machine, though he did not pick up the tube. "Oh, Maudie, you don't understand it at all. You don't get it. You put yourself in danger. You think the whole world is that college?"

"If I want to speak out, Dad —"

"Oh, shit," Stack said. "Speak out! Speak out! Stand tall! 'Lift every voice and sing, till earth and heaven ring.' Victory to the Vietcong! Those people don't come from where you come from. Not in any way, get it? You'll be the one that pays from riling up the religious fanatics and shitheads. It'll be you that pays! Whaddaya bet? Not some rich kid. Not one of these professors. You."

"Oh, thanks, Dad. Thanks for wishing me well."

"I mean, if they wanted to do that, how come they got a Catholic girl to do it?"

"Me? I'm not a Catholic girl."

"Sure, baby. Whatever you say. And speaking of professors, how come your adviser there, that guy Brookman, he's your adviser, he should have known if he has your interests at heart. Where was the advice? How come he let you?"

"Steve Brookman never saw it."

"Then he's not much of an adviser."

"I guess not," she said.

Stack picked up the tube of his oxygen tank, pressed the On button, inhaled and looked up at her. Not a kid anymore, he thinks. Not anyone's child. "He's your lover, isn't he? C'mon, Maudie, I don't get to see you much but I can tell by how you talk about him."

"You don't read my e-mail, do you?"

"Never mind. Listen," he said, "I want to tell you something. People's religion — it's not like opium. It don't work that way. It's their mother, you understand. They may not understand their mother at all. They may hate their mother. Maybe they're ashamed of their mother. Sometimes a mother makes someone hate other people. Any thing can drive such people to anything." He thought back for a moment and laughed a little. "When I started swinging a stick they told me: Put 'em in their place, tell 'em what shits they are, but for God's sake don't mention their mother."

"I don't care," she said. "I'm proud of what I wrote."

She thought: I can't stay here. He will be hurt and upset but I can't stay here.

So later that day, when he was out to a meeting or taking his walk, she packed her duffel bag and put on Shell's coat and went to Manhattan, where she knew some girls. When Stack returned he saw that she had gone. He was afraid and disappointed because he had thought she would stay over the holiday. At least he had thought that before the brouhaha over the article. Dizzy, he stayed on his feet.

"Barbara!" he called. Of course, every time Stack needed his wife, she was dead.

13

SHELL'S COLLEGE LIFE had lately taken the form of dodging the threatening calls and voicemail messages for Maud. Neither of them used the dorm room phone, but somehow or other someone had got the number. It was worse than after *The Harrowing of Hell*, when Shell had been compelled to change cell phone numbers again. And now it seemed that while people wanted to kill her and read about her being dead in the tabloids, they wanted to kill her roommate too, for more serious and worthy reasons. Three people had actually appeared at the dorm, gained access and entered in spite of the locks. All three were women; all three wanted to talk with Maud. So for Shell it was not only a matter of being herself but of being Maud's roommate. There were individuals and groups wandering the campus over Thanksgiving break, carrying signs about Maud. Maud, Shell thought, would never be able to cope.

An added thrill arose from the fact that the whole issue had afforded yet another conversion experience for Shell's insane ex-husband. The experience left John Clammer awash in insight.

John was able to understand now that the breakup of his marriage had been caused by Hell House — his name for the college — when it cleverly placed his wife with a demon adversary who had converted her to Lesbian Law. The enthusiast Clammer was organizing an expedition to rescue her, dead or alive.

An e-mail from her mother set out to explain the spiritual adventures of John Clammer. Shell was tired of trying to make sense of her mother's e-mails; interpreting her day-to-day speech was hard enough, but Shell thought her chances would improve on the telephone. She dialed her mother's number.

"Tell me quick, Mom. Is John Clammer still locked up?"

"Well, he is."

"You say he is?"

"Well, yes he is. But at times he isn't."

"Uh-oh. What times are those?"

"Well. John, they say, has this mentor, see."

"That should be good, Mom, 'cuz if any man could use a mentor it's John Clammer. Why do I have this feeling it's not an altogether good thing?"

"Well, there's this man and he's a preacher and his name is Dr. Russell Fumes. Dr. Fumes used to be the chaplain at that whole place when it was the great ol' state asylum, it was, and then of course it's just a teeny tiny place now and his cure of souls got just smaller and smaller. So Dr. Fumes was telling people, Now y'all be sure and tell the doctors that you need my coming round and how important it is. And they, I guess, they just didn't, or not enough of them did. So you know what was on his mind, he was thinking the hospital would stop paying him if he had no customers."

"I'm with you, Mom."

"Well, then he got John Clammer to accept the Lord as he sees 'um, and John told them he had to have this man Fumes. So Fumes come forward and says he'll take this man under his pastoral care and I guess they said cool because he's goin' aroun' with Dr. Russell Fumes."

"Goin' around with him? Where the fuck they goin' around to? Don't the court know I got a restraining order on that boy?"

"Well shit, honey, you don't see him around anywhere, do you?"

"I want you to make sure you know where he is, you hear! I know you can do that. Every couple days I wanna be reassured I can rehearse and perform and like that without having to shoot that sucker."

"Call your lawyer."

"I mean, that would look like hell, wouldn't it? I gotta shoot my crazy husband? Probably gotta shoot old Dr. Fumes too. Cute onscreen no more, Mom. I'll be a Fatty Arbuckle."

"Be what you gotta be, sweetie. He probably ain't interested in you no more. Everything ain't all about you no more."

of in the dark eyes of the young woman who sang with the montañeros.

A few days later, on a weekend evening, she was reading alone in the counseling office. The office was mainly below the sidewalk, but the upper third of the window commanded a view of the pavement, a drain full of frozen leaves and the footwear of passersby. When she had first taken the job years before, she had thought the office a strange place: a rather cast-down room in which to rouse depressed, confused or homesick students from their misery. For a while the counseling office had occupied the lobby floor of a downtown office building, sleek and sixties-modern. Now it had been shifted to this cellar of improvisatory afterthought. Owing to a confluence of ironies, counseling had been downgraded in the ranking nomenclature of the college.

There had been a time when students were simply expected to follow the rules and keep their own counsel. At the end of that era, the introduction of a dozen therapies, from gestalt to transformational breathing, collided with a crisis of confidence in these therapies, with extended individual rights and with the disappearance of in loco parentis as a defining relationship between institution and student. Then there was the expansion of legal liability. All at once it seemed that while nobody was responsible for anything, everybody was responsible for everything. In any case, Jo had low seniority in the counseling service and a subterranean chamber to go with it. But she had a following as a sympathetic presence, a word-of-mouth credibility passed along by students who managed to find her.

She had been at the desk with her uneasiness for a few minutes when the bell at the street door rang. Lone women—everyone—tended to proceed with caution around the college after dark. There were frequent buses and group safety routes. Jo went up the half flight of stairs to the street level and, looking through the solid glass doors at the building's main entrance, saw him on the sidewalk outside. A tall, thin man in his fifties with a scarred face stood in the lighted doorway. He was wearing a black beret, which he was stuffing into his overcoat pocket as he reached for the doorbell again. All the other offices in her building had closed and the street was winter dark. When he saw her through the glass door his eyes came alight. She let him in and gave him a chair in the office.

"I thought I saw you at the hospital the other day," she told him.

"Indeed you did. And I saw you, Josephine."

"Don't call me Josephine, by the way. Makes me feel like I'm married to Napoleon."

"Jo, is it?"

"Yes. Do we know each other?" How strange it would be, she thought, if this were the man she remembered.

He gave her face a long study. From his coat pocket he took a printout of one of the pictures from *Smith's Recognizable Patterns of Human Malformation* and a copy of the *Gazette* with Maud's article and picture.

"I thought there might be a chaplain's office. Then I checked the Newman Center. They directed me."

"I'm a layperson now. I withdrew almost thirty years ago. I'm on the counseling staff."

"Did you counsel Maud Stack?"

"That's confidential."

The man shrugged.

"She didn't seek counseling," Jo told him.

"Is she pregnant?"

Quite without meaning to, Jo gave him a look of disgust.

"None of my business?"

"I know you'd like to make it your business. Fortunately it's not, and you know it."

The man before her bore an uncanny resemblance to the one known as the Mourner. He had been the most extreme of those who embraced the option for the poor, the most avid defender of violent methods. He required approval, and more than approval he required power, moral and tactical. His way of exercising power was to become the fiercest of the revolution's priests. He took great risks with the government's death squads.

Like the Mourner, this man was long-faced, an inch or so over six feet, broad-shouldered but slender. He must have gone through repeated attacks of one kind of tropical fever or another that had left his skin discolored. His eyes were peculiar: swollen and mottled with flashes of unnatural light, outsize pupils, lids like flaking dirty lace. White men who lived in the lowlands under the montaña sometimes took on a look like that in the Mourner's eyes. Once his eyes had fascinated, with the power to halt a breath or a word. She could hardly believe she had not seen him before. But it was not possible, she thought. Everyone said the Mourner was dead.

This man's hair was white, trimmed closely and unevenly, possibly over a towel and a bathroom sink, but the effect suited him. The story was he had been badly beaten by the security police of several nations. Somehow the Mourner had got himself a reputation as a faith healer in one of the neighboring republics, a country traditionally hostile to the one whose regime he had been fighting to overthrow. Its security apparatus left him alone and he had begun to dabble in semi-miraculous cures. Jo had met him once at a conference at the Andrés Bello Catholic University in Caracas. At that time he was already a man to be feared.

After the movement collapsed and his excommunication was complete, he stayed in South America and became famous as a wilderness mystic who restored health to the lame, the halt, the virtually deceased. He took a beautiful mistress, choosing with brazen effrontery the daughter of a local hacendado, a brutal man whom he had appeared to cure of syphilis with indigenous potions and hypnotic spells. When the girl became pregnant he engaged the practice of abortion in a fearsome crusade, equipped with Genesis, Deuteronomy and a litany of terrifying curses committing sinners to the eternal service of Satan. His reputation extended to the tabloids of the capital in features read aloud beside shepherds' camps, in bandit caves and on river-borne canoes. His eyes were terrible, the eyes of a man of sorrows.

"Why did you come to this campus?" she asked the man before her.

"To visit Maud Stack. And to address her spiritual adviser. Someone needs to tell her that sometimes what we do when we're adolescents haunts us the rest of our lives. She may pay for it."

"Is that a threat, Father?"

He said nothing.

"In about half a minute," Jo said, "I'm going to call security. There's a surveillance camera in the hall outside."

"The least you could have done was raise objections. For the kid's own good. The thing she put in your newspaper! The blasphemy of it, Jo. So clever and so naive."

"I call that a threat," Jo said, but she made no move. She thought all at once of the raptor snake fixing its prey with a stare.

He treated her to his world-embracing smile. The smile that must have frozen the hearts of peasants when he arrived with his messages from the army of the people. The inquisitor of the proletariat come to show its suspected enemies the instruments. Quiet-spoken, with his educated diction and gentle clerical manner, he must have left the designated criminal element paralyzed with fear. And with remorse as well, overcome with repentance for whatever it was they were supposed to have done, ready to confess all night long to anyone ready to listen. Sometimes it took even longer before they could be made to comprehend what guilt was. In the end, everyone learned.

"Are you afraid of me, Jo?"

"I don't know why you came here. I need you to leave this office."

"I came to bear witness to murder and the mockery of Almighty God. To remind you of your duty."

"And I'm reminding you that you're trespassing here. You have no legitimate business on this campus and I'm letting our security know that you're threatening our students and staff."

"I'm not threatening anyone."

"Threatening our students and staff," Jo repeated. "I don't believe I caught your name. Father, is it?" She looked over the desk at him, pencil poised on a memo sheet.

"Just call me one of the mourners."

When she dialed campus security, he left quickly. The security chief was a middle-aged former national park policeman named Philip Polhemus. He arrived five minutes later accompanied by one of the young female officers. The college's police people wore military-style uniforms again after a decade or so of affecting comfortably academic blazers.

"We're keeping an eye open for him, Dr. Carr," Polhemus told her. "We'll make the city police aware of him. No clerical garb, right?"

"No clerical garb. He's shabby but clean-shaven."

"Let us know if you see him again and we'll escort him off campus. If he comes back we'll arrest him. Can you give us a description?"

"I'm sending you guys a memo," Jo told him. "He wouldn't give me a name."

In the memo to Polhemus she included his calling himself a mourner. It troubled her to invoke the words.

15

"GOOD LORD!" SHELBY SAID when she opened the dorm room door to Maud. "I can't believe you came back. How did you get here? Are you all right?"

"I walked from the station."

Shell took a step back and watched Maud drag her duffel in and collapse on their peeling leather couch.

"I got to tell you, baby, y'all look kind of drekko. I mean to say you're looking tired," she added.

"Yes."

"There's a sort of to-do, you know. Like we're getting death threats here. I mean," Shell said, "just like ordinary death threats like people get sometimes, the world being what it is. But still — death threats. Threats of death."

"I believe you, Shell. I don't think I give a shit."

"You know what? Miss Carr in the counseling office asked me to call her when you got back. If you got back. Or when, rather."

"The hell with her."

Shell folded her arms and looked at the door Maud had come through.

"I'm gonna call her. I'll take you to see her."

"Screw her," Maud shouted. "Fuck her. She's just gonna bitch about the thing."

"No, no. We need help. We need somebody to help us and she knows the scene. Like whether you should stay or go. What we should do."

"No!"

"Who do you want to talk to, sweetheart? Cops or deans or somebody? She's a smart, practical person, hear? You want to call her!"

It was after six in the evening when Jo got back to her office following Shell's call. On her desk she spread out the photographs that Maud had selected to accompany her article, the ones the *Gazette* had prudently declined to run. It took great effort to get past Maud's cruelty and folly in choosing them. The girl's mother had died before she had gone off to college. Her father had been called to the 9/11 scene. But the pictures Maud had proposed to impose on her enemies were so distressing—the gargoyle-faced, doomed little things described in medical Greek that sounded like science fiction. Welcomed to the breathing world like things under the spell of a bad fairy at the conception. The only consolation was that the worst of them soon died. Years before, in a school taught by nuns, Jo had heard a story about deformed creatures whose humanity was in question. It was an object of disputation whether these humanoid beings had souls. In case they did, it was said, Mother Church covered that angle, engaging an order of sisters to administer unimaginable measures of care to them. It was foolish, Jo thought, for people to expend their ignorant moralizing babble on this obscene and ugly quarter of theodicy.

But in fact Jo sympathized with Maud's calling the fanatics on their iconography. It was particularly strong-minded to pay them back in kind with the very sort of photos they liked to flourish. Not resisting the mockery had been the mistake. It took these privileged kids forever to see that not everyone inhabited the space they did. Hearing Shelby and Maud at the street door, Jo swept up the pictures and put them in a drawer.

Maud was wearing a plastic anorak against the intermittent rain. When Maud swept the hood off, Jo saw that her hair was unwashed, which was unusual. Her eyes were swollen, she looked generally untended, and she had alcohol on her breath.

"Want me to wait?" Shelby asked them.

Jo thought about it for a moment and sent Shell home.

"You're a good girl, Miss Magoffin. A good friend. Go home and go to sleep."

"You got us something of a perfect storm," Jo told Maud when Shelby was gone. "Where have you been hiding?"

"I didn't ask to see you. Shell said you wanted me here."

Maud sat down in the armchair in front of Jo's desk and wiped her face with one of the always available tissues on it.

"Would you not stare at me?" she said.

"Sorry. I bet you've been drinking a whole lot. Would you see a doctor up the hill for me?"

"I'm all right."

"Let's go up anyway. I'll drive you."

Maud shrugged.

Jo was friendly with a resident named Jeff Margolis, who she thought might be on duty that night. She called, and he was.

"Jeff, you very busy? It's Jo. I want to bring someone up to see you. I was hoping you could check her out and we could do the paperwork later. She's not injured that I can see but she's been drinking—probably a lot. She's well known around here."

Margolis asked Jo if it was Britney Spears or Lindsay Lohan. He pretended to believe that both were students at the college.

"I get 'em all mixed up," he said.

"I want to rest here a minute," Maud said to Jo.

"Promise you'll come with me?"

Maud nodded.

"Does your father know where you are?"

Another shrug.

"Can I call him?"

"Sure," Maud said. She let Jo trouble to look up the number. The man who answered sounded ill, and older than Jo would have expected. Jo told him where his daughter was and that she seemed all right.

Without further comment or perceptible emotion, the man thanked Jo for calling. Neither Maud nor her father chose to speak to each other on the phone.

Maud seemed steady as they walked up the block to the space where Jo had parked her Taurus. Jo brought the tissues along and put the box on the car seat between them.

"Why did you want to see me?" Maud asked as they drove. "Shell said you did."

"I thought because we got to know one another a few years ago we might have something to talk about."

"Like what?"

"Like how are you? Like what's going on with you?"

"Is this free? Like do I have to pay for you to do this?"

"I think it's covered, Maud."

"Did you want to talk about the thing I wrote?"

Jo laughed a little. "It was very forthright."

"I wanted it to be forthright."

"It made a lot of people very angry, of course."

"They don't know what they're angry about. They're tools."

"They're angry at having their faith ridiculed."

Maud turned to face her.

"There's not much wrong with the world that doesn't come from it having too many people in it."

"But Maud, the world *is* people."

"I thought it was mostly water."

"You're a wise guy," Jo said after a moment. "You're very angry yourself, right?"

Maud said nothing.

"When I was your age, I was very angry too."

"You were?" Maud said. "Hey, really? That's interesting."

"If you want to persuade people — I presume that's what you want — don't tell them they're fools."

"So who are they to put out all this intimidation? They're just looking for other people to push around."

"I have no beef with your opinion," Jo told her. "I basically share it. Did you think I was going to scold you for what you thought?"

"Isn't this what you're doing? Why are we having this conversation?"

"Two reasons, Maud. I want to see if you're all right, for one."

"I'm fine."

"Yeah? I don't think so."

"So mind your business."

"Look," Jo said. "People who think they have all the answers will always think they have a right to hurt people who don't believe them. That's the world, Maud. That's human nature."

"Why are you telling me?"

"Because you don't have to be quite so mean. You have a responsibility. Because you're smarter than most people. You go to a fancy school. Learn a little compassion."

"They have none," Maud said.

"May I ask you something, Maud? Did you ever have that procedure done?"

"I never had to. It didn't come up with me. Are you telling me I should shut up and let fanatics and heartless politicians take our rights away?"

"I'm not saying that," Jo said. It occurred to her, however, that arguably she was saying just that.

"I remember," Jo said, "when most women didn't have the choice to get it done right. My mom's generation." She turned to look at Maud's exhausted face. "Look, you pay a price for everything. Politicians don't give a damn and neither does the media. They make a living by keeping people muddle-headed and angry. You can't walk into this stuff without knowing what you're up against."

"I know that," Maud said.

"While you've been hiding out, there have been many threats against your life. You're in danger. You've got nuts after you. I mean," Jo said, "I'm not trying to scare you. Just be careful. Maybe — I don't know — you might take a semester off. Lie low."

"Fuck 'em."

"Whatever you want to do, Maud. Just be careful."

When they got to the hospital driveway, an orderly with a wheelchair was standing beside the admissions desk.

"I'll wait for you," Jo told Maud, and took a seat on a bench in the emergency department's waiting area. It was uncrowded. Sitting nearby was a student with a canvas leg cast that appeared to be causing her pain. It looked like a ski injury.

Less than twenty minutes after Maud had left her side, Jo saw Jeff Margolis, a thin-faced, goateed young man, coming toward her.

"Your Lindsay Lohan person flew the coop, Jo. She took off."

Jo stayed for a while on the bench pondering her next move, wondering if she had one. Finally she concluded there was nothing for her to do that night except drive home. She parked in her lot and got to her apartment just as it started to snow. She put herself to bed.

16

"So," ELLIE SAID. "This kid's a little genius, eh?"

Brookman saw that she had found the *Gazette* and read Maud's article. He had not been hiding it from her, nor had he brought it to her attention. However, he had left it in a downstairs drawer, thinking to keep it from Sophia. He assumed that someone on campus would contrive to mention it in Ellie's presence.

"Angry in all directions."

"Is she?" Ellie went to the window and looked at the street. Dusk was coming down. Outside, people had started to walk toward the ice rink where the college was about to play its opener against UConn. Prospects for the home team were not good. "Get over it, I say."

"It was immoderate. But she had a right."

"Oh, sure, she had lots of rights. In all directions." Ellie lowered the blinds against the passersby on the street just below and the strengthening reflection of the room they stood in. "Why did you let her publish it? She was your advisee, I understand."

"My advisee, yes. I hadn't read it."

"You didn't? Of course that's none of my business."

The words chilled him but he had no answer. From an intellectual perspective, even from an emotional one, he would have been interested in her comments.

"Pretty little thing," his wife said, observing the front page of the *Gazette*. "Beautiful, actually. Coltish. Sort of an uncontained animal spirit. Ah, youth, eh?"

She rolled up the college paper briskly, omitting to mention what she thought he might do with it. Whereupon she went upstairs. Brookman started to follow but stopped when he heard the bathroom door slam. Sophia was in her room reading *Are You There God? It's Me, Margaret* before bed. He began to drink. He read several chapters of a book about the decline of the Spanish Habsburgs and then reread some items from the previous day's *Times* sports section. One article described a Patriots-Broncos game that Denver lost. A Pats-loving colleague would have won fifty dollars from Brookman had the man not been off winter camping, out of cell phone range.

The liquor brought him no peace, only more anxiety and confusion. Finally he turned the television on and watched a sizable chunk of *Red River*. He realized that in the numerous times he had seen it, he had never figured out whether John Wayne shot John Ireland to death in their final encounter, nor had he ever remotely believed in the heroine's cool reaction to taking a Comanche arrow in the shoulder, despite Joanne Dru's feisty performance beside Montgomery Clift.

From the sidewalk outside he could hear the slightly intoxicated sounds of hockey fans coming from the rink. Amid the stomping, grunting and laughter there came a shout he recognized.

"Hey, Steve! Hey, Professor Brookman!"

He looked out and saw layers of snow gathering on the chestnut tree branches overhanging the curb. The heavy flakes whirled, driven by wind off the river a few miles away. At the foot of the tree stood Maud. She had on a bright plastic anorak that had lowered to her shoulders, and newly fallen snow was in her hair, as he had seen it weeks before. Her eyes reflected the light from his house.

A quarter mile away at the far end of his block, the doors of the hockey rink were open and spectators streamed out, most of them turning left as they exited, making for the main campus. A few dozen, in couples and small groups, were using Brookman's street as a shortcut. Maud clutched the sky-blue plastic cloth around herself and screamed at him, standing with her face to the weather, toward his house.

"Hey, Prof! Hey, Brookman! Steve!"

Ellie had come downstairs.

"What did you do," Ellie asked him, "give her a bad grade? Who is she?"

"She's one of the kids who drinks. Good student. Pain in the ass."

"Hey, Brookman!" Maud called from the street. "Who you talking to? Is that Mrs. Brookman? Hi, Mrs. Brookman." They heard what might have been a snowball or a piece of ice against the door. "Hi, Elsa! Congratulations there!"

Ellie turned to her husband.

"I know who she is," she said quietly.

"She'll wake up Sophia," said Brookman. Then, at a loss, he said, "Do you want me to call the police?" As he said it, he knew it had been a lame, stupid thing to ask her.

"The police," she repeated after him in a monotone. "I think not."

"Hi, folks," Maud yelled. "God bless your happy home."

He opened the front door and went outside, leaving it slightly ajar behind him. "Maud! What are you doing?"

She leaned the length of her arm against the tree trunk, turning to face him in the doorway.

"What am I doing? What am I doing, you son of a bitch?"

"You need to be sober, kid."

"Oh, Stevie, I am sober. I don't need anything. I am as sober as you've ever seen me, you dirty-hearted son of a bitch. You! Brookman!"

Cars maneuvered their way through the crowded street, sounding their horns, getting razzed and pounded on by the hockey crowd that was slow to yield the right of way. The street was normally closed on game nights. As the fans came abreast of Maud and Brookman, a few paused to look at the two of them, slowing the progress of those behind them.

Someone called Maud by name. A couple of passing boys

tried to grab her arm and made as though to carry her off, laughing. "Hey, come with us!"

Violently she shook her arm free.

"Am I making too much noise, Stevie sweetheart?"

Brookman put his hands out toward her, palms open. He thought his house door had opened wider behind him and took in a whiff of the kindly scents from inside. He turned and saw Ellie standing in the doorway.

Maud had caught sight of Ellie. She shouted at the top of her voice: "Are we disturbing the peaceful nest of your loving female duckies in there? Hi, folks! God bless your happy home, you assholes. Hey Miz Brookman, Miz Kiddo Brookman, everybody knocked up in there? You showing yet? I want to see."

A car passed, slowing down, its tires hushing under its brakes on the slippery asphalt. He looked over Maud's shoulder and saw the car's wobbly halt, an old Camry like his own. It took traction and sped on. There were more people on the street now, a few more lights around, passersby attracted or repelled by the melee.

"Stay inside," Brookman told his wife. When he ventured another look she was still in the doorway.

Maud took a step, a spring toward his door. He moved to intercept her. He had the sense there were more people around, more traffic. Moving hard, he put a low shoulder between his house and Maud, and that was when she started punching. Her first blow was a solid hook that turned his head sideways and came back elbow-first into his molars, which stopped him. Trying to stay up, he saw her charge, head down, almost succeeding in butting him, throwing an uppercut that missed.

More and more people gathered. Maud tried to pass him, feinted on one leg, made her move on the other. He kept his hands out, trying to keep himself between her and his front door. She let the plastic garment fall, wrapped it around her forearm and began to use it as a whip. He backed away and she charged him, punching with the anorak in her hand. Now her punches were heedless and, he thought, harmless, but one caught him on the side of his jaw. He lost his balance on the slippery sidewalk but stayed up.

"Maud! Please, Maud!" He was trying to shout down the violence of her attack.

Then she raised her head and wailed, shaking it from side to side, and she looked so piteous and stricken that out of lost love or mercy Brookman stepped out and took hold of her with both hands. The margins of the surrounding crowd withdrew; no one made a move toward them. Suddenly it seemed he and Maud were alone in the street, and a full rising scream rose from the crowd, getting louder and louder.

"Maud." He had lost his voice and could not raise it above the cry of the crowd around him. He was holding Maud and she was fighting him, both of them sliding on the sleety crust whitening the surface of the street. He could feel her bracing to run as the noise of the crowd grew louder. For a second he had a good hold on her, but she struggled free as if to run, and he grabbed her again.

People in the screaming crowd were shouting, "Watch out! Watch!" He heard Ellie shouting too. He looked over his shoulder and saw his wife come toward him, screaming too: "Watch out!"

Then Maud broke clean and turned, and as she did, an approaching car, like a black airplane, a thing out of empty space, tossed her in front of it. He would keep what he would always believe had to be a false memory of her falling like a booted Icarus out of a lighted sky in which there was somehow falling snow and her mouth open in a lovely *O* that had started to shape a word, and her long legs against the electric light, shooting out of the blue plastic square that rose like a kite lifting on a whirlwind and one of her boots flying what seemed the length of the block. She was gone for a moment. There was a hush, almost a moment of silence from the frenzied crowd. Then girls screaming. Boys screaming, and that was a strange sound you never heard on a baseball diamond or a soccer pitch.

His face was angled so that he took in, nearly saw, the blurred fishtailing of a dark automobile driven on, and on and off, the sidewalk at the speed of a night's winter light in snow. So fast, everyone said. Incredibly fast. One thing he was sure he saw: a very fat young woman in a ski jacket had made a move — maybe thinking to block the car — and then stopped like a cartoon creature arresting itself in midair and effecting a headlong dive away from the car's path, or what had been the car's path a fraction of a second before.

Maud landed partly against two brownstone steps and partly against the spear tips of the railing that guarded a house three doors down. The sound had the quality of a shattering and an element like brass resonating, a ring in it, a strange gong and a crack. Brass on bone, and blood, and screaming that echoed in the street. He was holding a mitten. Of all things he would think: A mitten, how utterly un-Maud-like a thing a mitten was.

Someone struck him hard and Ellie ran past him. She was running toward the bloodied child-figure that lay, wrapped tightly in bloody blue plastic, on the sidewalk.

17

JO WAS TRYING TO KEEP children's voices from ascending through the cloud cover that eternally shadowed the rain forest. It seemed impossible. She had forgotten all the sorcery of the place. To gather up the silver voices was like trying to gather the tiny fish at the edge of the river when your fingers would not close, like trying to gather tree and bird spirits in your mind. The effort made her whimper in her sleep. The glittering voices were above her as she rose out over the jungle's brown cloud and saw that they were drawing her to the base of the cliffs. She had always felt a thrill of fear encountering the cliffs on a trail.

The gorges loomed high and deep beyond measuring. Their rainbowed waterfalls and vast green shadows stifled effort or your pleas, reduced them to birdcalls. Never yielding, the gorges had the eagle's mercy, crushed and ripped your tiny beating heart. Voices drew her, and when they came against the rock they never broke but were changed and became a living cloud of harmonies, so sweet, so delicate, but so terribly queer, so alien. The cloud of voices then drew her up, not gently — violently, as in a fall, stopping breath again, up into canyons, past the last of thick-fleshed leaves and over the wall. The fear of it!

And there to her horror were the black lava meadows and the cruel blue sky and the thin clouds on the edge of the world. The disk of the sun, having risen to light silver fountains in the canyons below, to command a blazing moon, was disappearing now. The enormous thing the voices had become raced to the blackness overhead and the flash of the stars.

She thought it woke her but it was still the past, always the past. He was there. Around him only for a moment stood a ring of bronze children whose wary gemstone eyes were fixed on him. They sang to him and then were gone. She knew she was in her room and he was there. He sat on the edge of her bed and spoke to her in a mixture of Spanish, the languages of the montaña, luscious Portuguese, Papiamentu.

"What do you want?"

"To mourn."

Finally awake, she thought. But when she looked across the room she thought she could see him in the darkness. His face was drawn and bearded, as in the conventions of cheap religious art. His eyes seemed teary and dull but wetly reflected a wall lamp near the door.

"I'm the Mourner. I hear the silent screams."

El Doliente.

Her first and only experience of him had come at the beginning of her time in the montaña, when she was still in a state of

revolutionary exaltation. By now she had come to understand
the situation well enough to be very frightened of him.

"Call me Father Walter," he had used to say. He had been the
pastor of a Devotionist missionary parish in a province under
siege by the True Revolution. Little by little he had gone over
to them. Nor was it out of fear, although there would have been
reason for that. For a while, during his moderate-radical phase,
some in the English-speaking press, usually in North America,
referred to him as the People's Padre. Father Walter had found
that description congenial.

She remembered that he was once obsessed with sacrifices,
blood on the thorns, the power of the Infant of Prague, El Niño
himself. The Milky Way. No one could expound on the ideol-
ogy of the True Revolution more effectively. Even those who
failed to comprehend dreaded him. "Let them," he said, "who
are afraid of me be afraid for themselves." The People's Padre.
Now El Doliente, the Mourner, who heard the silent screams.

Her own trembling truly woke her. She cursed and went to
turn on the bathroom light and wash away her tears. In the mirror her youthful face. In the waking world outside she heard
sirens not far away. By now they were to her an almost reassuring sound.

18

ON A MILD DECEMBER DAY—so soft that on his rounds
he thought he could smell new grass and budding trees in the
park—Eddie Stack had just returned from his walk when a
New York police captain came to his door. The sight of the
senior man frightened Stack for a minute. He was no more at
ease when the officer took his cap off.

"Mr. Stack?"

Stack's daughter was dead, the victim of a nighttime hit-and-
run driver right off her college campus. Stack heard himself ask
the officer in, but the captain declined. Hit-and-run driver at
night. There would be information and assistance. The captain
gave him a folder with advice and instructions, a police chaplain's card clipped to it, and said something about Mrs. Stack
and prayers and it being personal to everyone in the job.

When the captain was gone, Stack walked to an armchair
with his blood roaring in his ears. His legs were failing under
him. He realized that things, his life and identity, had become

more different than he had thought the wildest compass of possibility could have afforded.

At first Stack could not believe it. Then, although he knew perfectly well what he had been told in the captain's soft professional tone, he kept thinking that the thing announced had been his own death. He had absorbed his wife's death by feeling that it had transported him into a kind of post-life of his own in which he was as close to her as to any of the living. Dying was frequently on his mind. He had the city's health care benefits but as a rule he did not go to doctors. Stack simply assumed that his emphysema and the damage he had done to himself by years of alcoholism were bills about to come due. It might be slightly premature — he was under seventy — but where he came from it was considered respectable in men. Now he tried to tell himself that he had been given notice. But Maud had no connection in his mind with death at all; her problems came from her insistent pursuit of living. Of the more abundant life her intelligence, her beauty and diligence, her courage, could win for her. During one of their constant arguments in past years she shouted at him:

"I have to live more of a life! I have to live inside a bigger circle than you and Mom did."

Trying to understand what he had been told, Stack was presented with a puzzle. Going off to the college, she had stepped out to the big circle. They rarely spoke after she moved up to Amesbury. When she came home to visit, she talked down to him. He beset her with cautions that he himself knew were cli-chés. So in that sense she was gone, lost to him. The other side of this was that she was a living part of him, someone who was so much of his mind and body that he could no more lose her and live than he could lose his heart.

In the gathering shock he felt his arms go numb. "My arms," he said aloud. When he sat down, the sensation went away but, holding his forearms in front of his eyes, it was impossible for him not to imagine his way back to the nights when his wife was working and Maud was a baby and he had carried her back and forth against his shoulder in the same room where he now sat, more or less dying. He would not let her do it, he thought. He stood up to run away, lurched back and forth in the room, swinging at phantoms, throwing elbow punches to free his arms of her. That was no good — it just brought back the memories and took his breath away and there was nowhere on planet Earth to run.

After the captain's visit, in terror of grief, to save his life, to humiliate himself, to undo time and death, to make a fool of himself unworthy of burning, he went out and bought a bottle to replace the one Maud had stolen. He thought he could catch fire more slowly with the whiskey but it made him violently sick in the downstairs bathroom. Then he drank more of it and was better.

Prompted by the whiskey, he fled up the stairs and stood for a few minutes at the door of Maud's room. Finally he could not enter, so he went to his own room and removed his Glock from a locked drawer and put in the clip. How stupid, he thought, to keep a weapon in your house unloaded. However, he knew why it was unloaded and not ready to hand as it should have been. He took the Glock downstairs with him. He had forgotten to go slowly on the stairs. Panting, he sat down again and poured more liquor. It was a waste, eight years of sobriety, but there was no way to put the stuff back in the bottle.

He stared at it, at the label. Jameson, the Catholic whiskey, as opposed to Bushmills, the Protestant. Some indeterminate rage had come over him, preferable to the pain. It was them, Catholics. Us. No, he thought. Them. They — them — had been many things over his lifetime — lawyers, perpetrators, judges, anyone they called mokes, civilians, the public in general, anyone who was not in the job. They had come to include just about the whole world now — the people who wrote the newspapers, the people you read about in the newspapers, the people who wrote letters to newspapers, the readers of newspapers. And television and its hypnotized witnesses. He had warned her about them and what would happen with the article. He had warned her they would hurt her. And she had become one of a different department of them, an anti-them, same thing, he thought, nutso fucks. He had tried to save her. But he himself was one of them because he was a drunk, a red-nosed clown, a fool.

And his own parents. And their parents. Them. His tee-totaler bartender father with the holy pledge to Matt Talbot, and his mother with her scented novena cards. Them. We ourselves. Too long sacrifice, yes. And we, they, quite probably, had destroyed Maud, the very people who begat the people who begat her. Finished ourselves off, our family, finished my rash young daughter and me. Too long sacrifice, to be sure. Burned our own house as always, in the name of ghosts.

God, he thought, she was right about all the pussy-faced bishops and slobbering priests. Maud had been right. She might just have broken our spell. He took out the gun's clip, looked at it and snapped it back in. Though it continue the cycle.

He woke, sick and breathless, the next afternoon feeling that grief, rage, alcohol and insomnia were likely to make short work of him, and soon. Then he thought with true terror of the grief that awaited him, the years of it he would have to endure. A grief that sooner or later would infest his heart and burn him down. All his love turned to scarring, a craze. Her childhood blotted out.

Downstairs, he drank ice water from the refrigerator until it eased his thirst and somehow steadied his heart. He still had the Glock semi-automatic he ought not to be in possession of. He had always thought of using a weapon against himself if the worst came. It would be nothing but shameful panic to turn it on himself so. He had seen, he thought, enough of that. It also occurred to him that it would be wrong to make so sudden and violent an end of Maud's memory, leaving no truly loving trace of her within the length of a day—girl gone, mother, father gone. It was not right. As to religious scruples, he had none. He drank more water and then had another swallow of the whiskey.

But as he had learned before, there were things to be done,

and one of them was to call the members of his family. The best person he could think of to handle it was his older sister Gerry, who had done it before. Gerry lived in Florida and passed the time there hating her wealthy ex-husband.

"Don't cry on me," he told her at first. He needed a tough cookie to pass the word.

He also called a former police surgeon named Sorkin, a friend of a friend, who would not give him barbiturates but called in a prescription for Ambien. The Ambien worked well enough for him to handle a call the next day from Gerry's despised ex, Charlie Kinsella, a dapper and much-feared former policeman. Stack feared Charlie as much as anyone and was not pleased to hear that Kinsella promised to drop by later in the day.

"Aw, God, Eddie," Charlie said when he came. He took Stack in his arms, affording him a whiff of his cologne. "I'm so sorry."

Charlie had his hair cut in a place that actors went to. He looked like an actor who might play an Irish cop on television and in fact had provided filmmakers with constabulary advice until even the most rash and reckless of the aspiring moguls had become afraid of him. Stack watched his former brother-in-law enter his living room with princely condescension. Stack thought he might actually be waiting to be shown a seat.

"Have a seat, Charlie."

Kinsella took off his overcoat in a way Stack thought showed every facet of the Harris weave. He had no idea what such an overcoat might cost. A thousand dollars? Five thousand dollars? More? The dark suit he wore was most impressive.

Charlie Kinsella took Stack's best chair, carefully removing the past week's newspapers from it, including a copy of the *Gazette*. He rested his resplendent overcoat over an adjoining rocking chair, leaving the sofa to Stack, and looked around the room.

"No pictures of Barbara?" He spread his hands, almost smiling, seeming really to require an answer.

"No pictures."

"I put them up myself, pictures of the departed. I'm not afraid of living in the past."

I must show nothing to him, Stack thought. Not a wariness of the eye nor a flicker of tongue to lips. Nor the rage he felt at the sound of his dead wife's name on the thin lips of this man who could dazzle her with a glance, before whom she blushed and melted from shame. Who can freeze me with undifferentiated fear in the throes of my grief when I care nothing whatever for living.

Stack thought he knew where the coat and the cloth of his suit had come from. From an expensive tailor's shop he was reasonably certain could not be far from Ground Zero on the flame-lit night of the day in question.

"Yez should keep a picture of Maudie."

"I don't think so, Charlie. Wouldn't put one up for a while, I believe."

How crazy he was, Stack thought. How foul he was! That he should refer to my lost child as "Maudie." For many years, between the time Maud was a small child and an occasion when she was almost grown, Charlie had not seen the girl. And when introduced to the young adult Maud, he had taken her hand and looked into her eyes with astonishment. Stack knew why. Because Charlie had seen there the youthful married Barbara whom it had been his delight to seduce and perhaps even display once or twice to his hoodlum company, to her mortification.

So Maud had met him. And after meeting him she had said, "Oh, my God. This man is *my uncle!* He says 'yez.' He says 'I ain't.' He's a cretin!"

And Stack had said, "The word is troglodyte."

Stack and his daughter had had a laugh. But Charlie was not a troglodyte or a cretin. He was of the rarest.

Kinsella's eye fell on the bottle of whiskey Stack had not troubled to put aside.

"Oh no, Eddie. This is not the way."

"Fuck you, Charlie. I mean, go fuck yourself, Charlie." His adding the second part risked making Charlie Kinsella cross.

"I think I know how you feel," Charlie said. "You said this thing was a hit-and-run?"

"That's what I was told."

"They get him, it might be resolved. To some satisfaction. They get him, he's ours, Eddie."

Stack let it pass, but a similar thought had not spared him.

"Gerry was a lot of help to me when Barbara passed."

"Certainly you can count on her," Charlie said curtly.

They sat in silence for a moment.

"Listen, Eddie," Charlie Kinsella said. "There isn't a chance that in the recovery operation somebody misunderstood something? That something got out and some fuck saw it wrong?"

"You mean heard something and hurt Maud?" Stack stared at him. At first he failed to grasp what Kinsella was asking him.

"You didn't hear about what she wrote?"

"Yeah, sure," Charlie said. "But I thought just to eliminate . . . you know."

"You know I didn't touch that shit, Charlie. You know that!"

So the evil of Kinsella and Stack's own weakness caused the shadow of the dark side to flicker over his grief. The man was suggesting Maud was struck down in vengeance for a guilt that never touched her. Or so lightly. So hardly at all.

"As though I ever fucking referred to it. You're crazy."

Charlie did not see himself as crazy. Ever.

Many understood that more personal possessions — cash on a primitive level, credit cards, financial documents, keys and codes, little things and larger things — were found in the dreadful ruins of the twin towers than could ever be returned or passed along or released in an orderly manner to every one of the survivors, if any. Many understood that early in the day on September 11 a brutal, lawless element accompanied the responders, requiring, demanding a share of what was gathered up in that inferno. It happened all the time. It was the world. It was mere humanity.

Old criminal conspiracies that had been, so to speak, present in the pilings under the river, the shafts, the salt-encrusted drowned alleys and bricked-up tunnels, with the eels' nests and the wrecked rope walks — that had been there in spirit since the first white men, with their bindles and kit, and before them — had emerged with the fire coming down. The word had gone out. Competing villainies saying, It's ours. Nobody ever suggested such a thing was common or general or even frequent. It was despised and aberrant. Still, it happened.

In depraved quarters, greed and suspicion. "We said all. All over a certain figure. We said all what yez got!" Were all your average citizens a hundred and fifty percent better? No way! So mistakes were made. Charlie Kinsella and associates had a crust. A crust and maybe a crumb besides. It wasn't more.

Eddie Stack was present that day. His share was emphysema. Placed where he was, he knew a little of what was going on. He could no more have picked up some poor lost soul's posthumous possession than he could have plunged his hand into a molten girder or into the guts of some poor woman who might have been his own wife or daughter. It was impossible not to half know it, in flashes and fits and the edge of vision, at the rim of a policeman's mind. And of course there was his then brother-in-law Charlie Kinsella. Stack never saw him that day, but Charlie was there.

Days later the smoke was still everywhere, seeming to be the only source of light. Stack was beginning to understand that he would never draw his breath as before. Maud was safe in her classy Catholic boarding school, where the nuns were long gone but underpaid youths of the Ivy postgraduate faculty struggled to balance the tragedy of the city's martyrdom with the understandable grievances of the Third World. Barbara had been dead and gone for more than a year, but he still talked to her and still felt she heard him. Then appeared what some old party in an immigrant past might call "a wee man"— sure enough, a little fellow. A little Pinocchio face of a guy. He looks like UPS but he's not. He's wearing a messenger's uniform but you look at his mug, Stack does, and sees not a messenger in the usual sense. He's come in a panel truck and there are two men with him, not messengers either. The small man has a big box.

So the guy says, "I come from Charlie K."

And Stack is so confused he thinks, What is that, a Chinese restaurant? but just as well doesn't say that, or anything. The man at the door's impatient and thrusts the box at him. It's medium heavy. Stack struggles to hold it.

"Charlie," the man says, lowers his voice.

"Charlie Kinsella." Leaning on the *K,* what Maud would call a plosive, almost ending the word with an *s,* which she'd call a sibilant. "Keep it very safe. A day. Maybe two. Be here. Stay with it."

When the guy's gone, Stack is so rocked he's merry and he makes a black joke to dead Barbara.

"Can I open it?"

God only knows what's in the box he stays inside with, missing his doctor's appointment, until the same man comes back for it. He knows what's in it. He doesn't know what's in it either.

The following year, Maud's admitted to every college he's ever heard of. She's got the National Merit Scholarship and financial aid up the gazoo — the guidance counselor at the classy Catholic school helped arrange this. In the end, she picks the college in Amesbury, one of the top liberal arts schools in the country.

It is a great relief to Stack that so much aid is being supplied because it is all unbelievably expensive. And beautiful Maud wants clothes and presently, over her freshman year, will want other things that college girls have, and money for travel and so on.

One day there arrived the man himself, Charlie Kinsella.

"Listen, Eddie, I just wanted you to know we know you got expenses, and we really thought, This man helped us and we should help him. Because I know you're a guy who thinks, you know, and I don't understand half the fuckin' words you say, it was the same with Barbara, God rest her soul — educated — and the kid's gonna be more so, right? So we wanna help."

"I . . . I'm good, Charlie. Seriously, brother, I'm good. We're good."

Kinsella shows no sign of leaving. He looks very assured in his new clothes. He's very assertive.

"We want to give you something. We want yez to take it."

"Really, Charlie, I don't want anything."

Charlie K. makes a pained face. As one on the horns of a dilemma.

"Um," he says, "I don't lie to the people I work with. Everybody knows that. They know that. Never."

"Right," says Stack.

"Anyweez," he says in a rollicking fashion, "I gotta be able to tell them we helped you out. You see what I mean?"

As much as to say, Stack thought, that there was no way around it.

Stack was reduced to shaking his head, as in no. Kinsella let him understand that the "something" offered was cash. "Nobody's," Kinsella said, which Stack inferred to mean unmarked. It was nowhere to be seen on that visit. But Stack mercifully would have no more of such packages or of the unspeakable Charlie until — until now, Maud dead.

What had happened was this. Maud's college career indeed called for more expenses than might have been foreseen. Charlie Kinsella had a son, Michael, from his first family with Stack's sister Gerry. Michael practiced law in Florida and might one day be a young champion of conservative forces in that state. The attorney administered a fund for the purpose of paying whatever expenses Maud Stack incurred during the term of her education and the years of her setting forth in the world. The bills and such were passed along and Michael Kinsella wrote checks to meet them in order that Maud not be denied the full enjoyment of the opportunities presented her by a fine education at a world-famous seat of learning.

Now here was Charlie suggesting some fuck saw it wrong.

"Would I know anything, Charlie?" Stack asked. "Would something come from me? What could I say, for God's sake!"

He saw that his protestations had convinced Charlie and also curled his lip very slightly.

"Sure, Eddie," Kinsella told him with a punch on the arm. "Yer a standup dude."

19

LIEUTENANT LOU SALMONE saw her for the first time on the pathologist's table at the hospital. The spoiled beauty of the young woman laid out there moved him in ways he could not have written down and would never dream of trying to express. The ambient smells were those usual to an autopsy room, and the mixture of mortified humanity and disinfectant somehow conveyed a judgment. The table on which she lay was made of stainless steel. It was a calamitous fall from grace. Bad luck, sure, but you could see and breathe punition and guilt. It made you suspect that what they said might be true, that somewhere in time, maybe ages before, somebody must have done something to make this happen to people the way it happened to cats and dogs.

The wise guys always pointed out how you had to have at least two people to have a murder. A famous person had said, "Character is fate." This was the wise-guy version: A person had made a mistake, they liked to say, and somebody had to pay. They didn't give a damn about justice, only about restoring their version of the natural order. The victim was always at a disadvantage, being dead and so often unsightly.

The kid had been lying half in the road, half on the sidewalk, her upper body wrapped to the neck in sky-blue plastic, her head turned at an impossible angle, legs twisted under, one tapering to a boot, the other stocking-footed. Everything about her position on the sidewalk had been incompatible with life. Deeply dead, she had looked.

Deeper dead now, naked on the table beside where Salmone stood. A yoke supported her neck, to hold her head up to the light. It looked distinctly like a temporary expedient to keep her facing the inquiries of the breathing world before what remained of her was put aside.

The examining pathologist was a short, neat man called Dr. Patel. Her ID, what old-time cops called an aided card, stated the victim was Maud Mary Stack, a student at the college from New York City who lived on campus. According to Dr. Patel's preliminary record, she was six feet tall, weighed one hundred and twenty pounds, was well nourished and athletic. The hospital pictures of the corpse showed Maud's pale freckles. The EMTs had cleared small traces of ethanol vomitus from her mouth. Her blood alcohol content was .20. Fluorescence revealed no semen on her body or her clothes.

Maud's belongings were in a plastic evidence bag but would not give evidence of much. She had credit cards, a driver's license, a New York MetroCard. Forty-six dollars in bills and coins. No cell phone, which was strange. There was a worn birthday card in her jeans pocket with no signature. On it was a single line in what would prove to be Maud's handwriting: "Dear heart, how like you this?"

"Her neck was broken," Patel said. "Skull fractured. Practically all the ribs on the left side. Vertebrae. Internal damage, so she won't be an organ donor."

"Freakin' destroyed," Salmone said.

"So how fast was this driver going?"

"What do you think?"

Patel shrugged and smiled faintly. "Nobody saw this car?"

"None of the witnesses gave much of a description. Just that it was big and fast."

"Well," Patel said, "the state is sending a guy down who does traffic deaths for a living. Sometimes he can make a case for a match between a specific vehicle and a specific injury without blood or tissue. For what it's worth."

"Tell the state's guy to look for wounds or bruises might result from an assault," Salmone said. "She was in an altercation just before the car hit."

"I don't know about that. She was knocked all up and down the street, against steps and gates, et cetera. He'll have a look."

Salmone was not sure he had ever seen Maud Stack on the campus; it was not a place he frequented. He did know that his friend of many years ago, Eddie Stack, had a daughter there. Salmone knew many people throughout New England, and it was not a rarity for some of them to have children at the college. In Stack's case, though, her death touched on a friendship from the days when Salmone had started his career as a New York City patrolman, before his father had retired and the police department in Amesbury made a pitch for Salmone to take up the stick there. In fact, hizzoner the mayor himself had extended a kind of invitation. Salmone did it — a move that involved enormous economic, moral and familial complications — because he had thought it was the appropriate thing to do.

He had done it for his elderly parents and because his wife, who grew up in Amesbury, had family and friends there and disliked New York. Salmone's mother had died soon after the move. His father had lingered long. He was a busybody, a loud-mouth, an invalid, a professional Friend of the Mayor, friend here, friend there, everybody's fucking friend, until Salmone grew to hate him. And Salmone's wife, who had to move back to town so as not to have to bring their children up in dread in New York, walked — divorced him, turned his very children against him. Even his venal father was shocked.

"She wasn't really Italian," the old guy would say helpfully. "She was an Albanese, a gypsy witch. That family was from Puglia, they wasn't even Catholics." Whereupon he would make useful signs against the evil eye.

So Salmone was left to live in the Little Italy of the college's town, where few Italian Americans remained and where many people from the state of Durango, Mexico, lived and labored. Which had left Salmone to a dissipated and troubled small-city-constabulary middle age from which he was still recovering. That he was now standing by the corpse of the child of a man who had once been a friend, whom Salmone had been in the job with and partnered with, struck him in ways that were confusing but somehow familiar.

On his way back to the station he stopped at the scene of the accident. The scene also happened to be the area of Felicity Street directly outside the front door of the professor on whom Maud Stack had come calling on the night of her death. The responding officer's report had described her as exiting the house, but it had turned out that she had gone there and been refused entrance by the professor and his wife. The girl was drunk, according to the professor — the toxicologist at the hospital supported him in that — so the professor had not let her inside.

Salmone had found the professor's statement of very limited usefulness. She had come to his house, he had offered, because she was his student — his advisee. But he had shed no light on why she had come there crocked at eleven o'clock at night. Also on his reason for not letting her in on that particular night. And why exactly they were reportedly having other than friendly physical contact in the street subsequent to her visit. Among other things not illuminated.

She had raised hell and the professor had gone out to placate her or otherwise persuade her to leave. The whole ruckus had taken place in front of a crowd leaving Collier Rink after a hockey game, and the car that hit Maud had come out of that crowd, injuring a couple of other students and leaving Maud dead in the street, almost on impact. Salmone had statements, taken by other officers, from the professor and his wife. He had other statements, taken from witnesses and first responding officers, and he had spent part of the day reading them. A number of students, three particularly vociferous, claimed they saw Professor Brookman deliberately push Maud Stack into the path of the oncoming car. The city police had statements and a number of cell phone videos that might be used to support that charge. But the people in the crowd had argued about it and the majority of witnesses affirmed that what they saw was Brookman trying to pull Maud Stack out of the car's way. A lot of the videos could equally well be interpreted to show that. Salmone decided to look at the statements and the videos again. He thought he might bring some of the witnesses in again as well.

At the curb a few doors down, he ran into Philip Polhemus, the college's chief of security, a highly regarded man who had retired from the U.S. Park Police. Polhemus still had a youthful, outdoorsy quality about him — longish gray-blond hair and a full bushy beard that the college would have figured would make him congenial to student-age elites. But the beard vaguely annoyed professional police officers. Polhemus was standing in the street with a camera.

"What are you taking pictures of, Philip?" Salmone asked.

Looking around, Salmone could see a few blood spatters on the curb, boot prints and a museum of tire tracks. The ones that might have been relevant were on the sidewalk, but the snow had melted and they had deteriorated. If anyone had measured or photographed the treads, he hadn't heard about it. Amid the soiled slush lay some of the plastic instrument wrappings the medics had tossed. Television crews had left some disposable equipment stacked on one of the house rails.

"Who knows what, right?" Polhemus said. "The dean is very upset. This street was supposed to be closed for the hockey game. Somebody moved the barricade. The No Entry sign is gone."

"That's trouble," Salmone said.

"He's going to want to talk to you soon."

"Me? Since when am I in traffic?"

"Don't you know who the dead girl was?"

"Maud Stack," Salmone said. "She was the daughter of a guy was my partner once in NYPD."

Polhemus moved closer to Salmone and lowered his voice.

"She was the girl who wrote the anti-religious stuff in the *Gazette*. The stuff against the abortion protesters."

Salmone just looked at him.

"Remember we had like a hundred demonstrators? You guys made some stops checking license plates. Well-known anti-abortion people. They came from all over. TV cameras."

"I don't read the *Gazette*," Salmone said. "I remember the big demonstrations, but I was out sick."

Salmone read neither the *Gazette* nor the daily papers. He had given up on television except for watching sports in their season. There had been some kind of anti-abortion hassle during the time he was having his gall bladder out at Whelan, and he remembered some talk in the corridors, but he had tuned it out.

"Anything to do with this Professor Brookman?"

"She was a special student of his. She died right here." Polhemus pointed to the Brookmans' college-owned Federal. "In front of his house."

"Right," Salmone said. "The dean hasn't called me."

"He will. I'll be in touch."

The police station lived in one wing of City Hall, a nineteenth-century Neo-Renaissance copy of a German *Rathaus*. There Salmone looked over the cell phone videos from the scene of the incident again. A dozen state troopers, within whose competence such things seemed to lie, had spent a large part of the day watching the videos sequentially on a widescreen monitor, without getting a make on the car or driver.

The videos were jittery, drizzly and snow-blown. What they focused on up to the very last was a one-sided shouting match, ending in a brief scuffle between a girl recognizable as the late Maud Stack and a large, short-haired man who would have been Steven Brookman. More students insisted that Brookman had tried to save her life than said he had pushed her toward the car. But every one of the videos ended in a scattering, a rushing disorder and dissolution of images. In the end, it was impossible to determine positively what had taken place.

One student had brought a camcorder, equipped with sound, to the game and afterward had filmed some of the encounter between professor and student. The footage was disturbing.

There were terrified screams, and it was just possible, if you knew how to listen, to hear a voice calling out, "He pushed her." But the video showed no such thing. Frenzied bodies blocked any view of the speeding car. And the student statements mainly had Brookman to the rescue, too late.

The three students who claimed to have seen Brookman push her seemed very convinced and irate. Salmone decided to call them. They stuck by their stories.

"Yes," one of them, a boy, insisted. He might have been a little overwrought. "I'm absolutely certain, he practically picked her up and put her under the wheels." On paper, his words looked solid. On the phone, he sounded like a screwball. Still, the Brookman person troubled Salmone. He hadn't liked the sound of the wife much either. No one, except maybe the Staties if they made the car, was going to the district attorney. Salmone thought he owed a call to Eddie Stack.

20

Salmone had no success contacting Stack during the rest of the day. In between his attempts to call, he read the article in the *Gazette* that had caused all the trouble. It was insulting, insulting in a particularly smart-ass way, more than the simpleminded badmouthing shit a perpetrator might say and get his sentence enhanced. Why should a kid use all that education just to belittle someone's religion when it might be all they got? Sometimes the college could be an incredibly mean place; when the kids reflected it they had the sharp language and the intelligence but no sense and no mercy.

But the grossest thing was not the mocking tone of the article. The grossest part was the color photographs of abnormal births that abortions, Maud Stack believed, were meant to prevent. The pictures weren't in the paper, but apparently she had meant them to be and they'd gone out online. The worst one Salmone saw was the baby with Meckel-Gruber syndrome. The big-headed one. It was really fucking ridiculous: church people, anti-church people, marching around with monster pictures to make each other sick.

At ten o'clock the next morning, he got a call from Polhemus telling him that Dean Spofford would appreciate his stopping by College Hall.

"I always have time for the dean," Salmone told him.

It was a nasty, sleety day, the kind of day that aroused in Salmone vague fantasies of retirement in Puerto Rico, a place he had visited once with some gambling friends who liked to stay at places like the Isla Verde Sands and the El San Juan and lose their money. It was all very sleek and brassy and sunsplashed, quite unlike coastal New England, where, he was fairly certain, he was going to spend his remaining years.

Polhemus was waiting for him under the white-painted arch at the College Hall steps. The dean's office, on the third floor, could be reached by a winding stairway lined with the portraits of collegiate notables past or, more practically, by the mandatory elevator, which was said to have entrapped a few of those notables. The former park policeman headed for the stairs but checked himself and rode up with Salmone.

"It's a tragic thing when a young person dies," Salmone said.

"Family to us," said Dean Spofford, which was what he'd said the last time.

John Spofford was slight and actor handsome, though not in the least epicene. His physically unruffled appearance was a concession to his job; he would actually have been more at ease with his hair less barbered and combed, in a less well-measured and expensive suit. He would not have insisted on looking younger than fifty-one, which was his age.

"Yes sir," said Salmone.

Everyone shook hands on it. The dean offered them chairs and said nothing, then, about the street that was supposed to have been closed.

"I understand that Maud was leaving the Brookman house," Spofford said.

Polhemus let Salmone answer.

"She never went in the house, Mr. Spofford. They stood outside and allegedly caused a disturbance. That's our understanding."

"So Professor Brookman came out."

"Correct. And his wife — Mrs. Brookman — followed him out just before the car."

"Nothing on the car?"

"Not as yet, as far as we know."

"The state troopers are hard at it, close on it," Polhemus said. "We understand the governor called."

"An alumnus," Spofford said. "Think it was an anti-abortion fanatic?"

Salmone gave him a small shrug.

"Certainly possible. The snowstorm, the way everything happened, that's made it very hard for us with the car."

"An unexpected car," said the dean. Polhemus began to answer, but Spofford interrupted him and addressed Salmone.

"So tell us about the Brookman business."

Salmone had brought his notes.

"Approximately eleven p.m., just before the game gets out. It's snowing. Miss Stack appears outside Mr. Brookman's house. She yells his name. Maybe throws snow at the window. Gets him out there. He comes out. They argue in an agitated manner. Finally they're in maybe a shoving match. She's yelling. He's maybe trying to calm her but he's been drinking too. They both were intoxicated."

"But not drinking together?" Spofford asked.

"Not at that time, because she didn't go in the house."

"Sounds like a lovers' quarrel, though," Spofford said.

Salmone said nothing.

"I mean," said Spofford, "I guess there's no reason to assume that. Do you think a crime might have been committed in this melee?"

"We're pursuing the circumstances of the incident, Mr. Spofford. All the surrounding factors."

"Going to talk to students?"

"We would normally do that. Students and faculty and staff."

Everyone sat in silence for a moment.

"So, Mr. Polhemus," the dean said, "you'll help him out?"

"We've set up some interviews," Polhemus told him.

"Experience shows — I believe — that they're more comfortable if we go to them."

"To dorms?"

"To dorms and college locations."

"If possible," Salmone said.

Later that day, Polhemus accompanied him to a student lounge where they could talk privately with Shelby Magoffin. Dean Spofford went off to deal with the media effects of Maud's death, which everyone knew would complexify as the hours passed. Salmone was grateful that the media fallout would devolve, for a while, on the Staties, who handled road accidents as a matter of routine.

Salmone's encounters with Dean Spofford always refreshed his current understanding of how things stood in Amesbury. The city force had endured a few embarrassing scandals over the years and did not enjoy total confidence in the high places with which most college students connected. There were also some confusions of history, different perspectives on the class struggle. Many people thought the issues dated from some violent incidents in the sixties, but in fact the hostility went much further back. Nearly a century before Vietnam, students in Brooks Brothers tweed had gathered to throw snowballs at the cops marching in Amesbury's St. Patrick's Day parade or some other celebration. Pranks the rich kids thought droll roused ancient hatreds in the immigrant-descended police. The town-and-gown business in the city had always been bitter, and was more so when the factories closed.

The city obliged the college beyond the limits of necessity, but the old pols who could not learn the diction of enlightenment disappeared from public life. The college was the only thing in town left standing and was increasingly less polite about having its way. Distinctions of class and identity persisted. Lieutenant Salmone had grown up in a police family and understood all this well.

The public had the impression that screwy things did not happen around the college end of town, but any officer knew better. You could ask the campus cops about the weirdness they dealt with. There were bomb threats and threats of other kinds. Bad fistfights, duels, accusations and denials of date rape, unquestioned rape, thefts. Occasionally grand larcenies like the priceless Persian carpet removed from the dean's office, a particular embarrassment. The museum once lost an oil by a fairly well-known follower of the Hudson River school.

Most of the campus cops' reports, however, were the stuff of amusing stories. The unamusing ones were conveyed to parents through Dean Spofford, who was assigned to deliver grim tidings. The substance of these were along the lines of: Your son was on acid; he thought he could fly. Or: Your daughter OD'ed on smack, pills, vodka. Sometimes the news would be too bizarre or tragically ludicrous to be explained over the phone, in which case Spofford would find a way to duck it.

When a student was murdered, an event that occurred once or twice a decade, the perpetrator was often what the thoughtful referred to as a young community male. The police referred to such people as dirtbags. A dirtbag might be a crackhead from one of the dead mill towns up the valley, or a ghetto kid from the far side of any street that took you anywhere. He might even be from one of the old neighborhoods like Salmone's. The new century was short on promise for townies. Some dirtbags were solitaries but most of them ran in packs. They tended to get loaded and talk too much, whereupon the dime, as the old expression had it, would drop. Salmone would get the call and usually the state would get a conviction. The less said about that, the better.

When the suspect, usually the killer, was a student, circumstances differed. The college maintained a pretty professional security service that often knew a surprising amount of what was going on around campus. Normally the officers made use of less than they knew. Most of the problems they had to deal with were trivial kid stuff. Sometimes things got serious, as in the theft of the carpet — a prank theft by nihilist art students but nevertheless grand larceny of an object worth hundreds of thousands of dollars. Intramural murder was something else. Law enforcement had to tread carefully, and rarely even in the bad old days did a city cop take the end of a telephone book to a student suspect. And no more rubber hoses, even for dirtbags.

The Common was no longer under snow as Salmone and Polhemus walked across it. They followed the path that was being cleaned by men in Day-Glo vests, chiefly offenders performing their community service. The sleet had given way to a pale blue sky edged with cirrus clouds; the lower storm clouds were heading inland for the hills. It was getting noticeably colder again.

They talked about the weather most of the way across. Polhemus, it turned out, knew about all sorts of weather — tropic, arctic, subtropic, subarctic. The park service had kept him on the move, having to relocate his family almost every two years, and there were parks in every climate zone. He told Salmone he had started out as a ranger but transferred early to the park police to keep his job.

"They want us to quit," he told Salmone. "They want to do away with the parks. Wait and see, Sal. Not one national park in America will ever be two hundred years old. The Congress thinks they were a terrible idea."

"People get hurt in the parks," Salmone said.

21

WHEN THEY GOT TO CROSS INN, Salmone put a hand on Polhemus's shoulder to make him pause.

"Brookman seems like a guy who might have a lot of girlfriends."

"That's what I hear," Polhemus said. "It's not allowed but nobody snitched on him."

As they went inside, Polhemus told him a little about Shelby Magoffin, that she was a professional film actress and a little older than she looked.

"She has a bad-ass husband down south she has a restraining order on. Which I don't even know is enforceable in this state outside our property. She has a few overenthusiastic fans. She's semi-famous. We haven't had any real trouble."

They talked to Shelby in a small paneled room, cleared and curtained for the purpose. Polhemus stayed but left all the questions to Salmone.

"Can I call you Shelby?"

"Of course," she said. "Yes, sir."

"You weren't with Maud when she died?"

"No, I sure wasn't."

"Where were you?"

"Where was I? I was right here. I was sleeping, I believe."

"Was Maud having an affair with Mr. Brookman?"

"You know," Shelby said, "it's hard for me to talk about her personal affairs so soon." She let it rest there, and Salmone wondered if she would talk at all. Finally, she asked, "Is that relevant?"

"We think it might be."

She took off the white scarf she had been wearing and wrapped it so as to cradle her elbows. She was elfin-faced, big-eyed, looking guileless.

"I don't get it," Shelby said. "Why?"

"If we knew, it would help us. We're working for her now."

She looked at him with patient contempt, a waif no longer.

"Yes, sir. It seemed like she was in love with Mr. Brookman because he had seduced her last year."

"When you last saw her the other night, she was on her way to his house?"

"I guess so."

"Could you tell us her mood at that time?"

"Real upset," Shelby told him and, to his surprise, started to cry.

It put him on more familiar ground. He moved toward her a little and let her see his eyes.

"Was she angry?"

Shelby took the scarf from around her arms and touched a tear with it.

"Yeah. Angry, hurt, left … All those things. His wife had come back. Coming home pregnant like the best of all possible wives, bearing him kiddies. So he was ditching Maud. He was breaking up with her. Like cutting her loose, goodbye, like that."

"Would you say she was intoxicated?"

"Yeah. Intoxicated."

"How angry was she? Angry enough to be violent if she was intoxicated?"

"Nothing violent about Maud. Drunk or sober." Shelby slid into a posture vaguely based on Maud's. "She was demonstrative in her own space. She was verbal."

"What did you think about Brookman?"

"Oh, everybody likes Brookman, sort of. Big lovable rogue of a guy. Incredibly hot. I liked him at first. Then I thought about it and I had to feel bad for Maud. Married guy, kids, big talker."

"Did she ever come back injured? With a bruise?"

"Huh? No!"

"He have a lot of girlfriends besides Maud?"

"Over time I guess he did. I think he was the kind of guy who took 'em one at a time."

"But like you say," Salmone said, getting a little intrigued with her, "he was married."

"Sure, there had to be the wife. Then he had to go out and be adored. He wasn't that promiscuous, not by the standards of this place."

Salmone, faintly surprised, glanced at Polhemus. Polhemus shrugged.

"So you don't think there was another young woman somewhere?"

"I'm sure there wasn't."

"How about Maud? Did she have a boyfriend? Did she break up with another student over Brookman?"

"Not while I knew her."

Salmone thanked her courteously for her time. She was very fidgety by then, her big innocent eyes blinking and looking for corners.

"Who should we talk to next?" Salmone asked her.

"I don't know," Shelby said. "Maybe Jo Carr at counseling. Maud was gonna see her after she left here."

"What time was that?"

"A little before ten, maybe."

"Late for counseling."

"Miss Carr wanted to see her. Well, I think Jo Carr knew about the situation. She had an interest in Maud."

"An interest how?"

"Miss Carr had counseled Maud in her first two years. Might have been Maud took her problems there sometimes."

Polhemus and Salmone thanked her again and she walked quickly toward the main lounge.

"Hey," Shelby called over her shoulder, "think maybe Mrs. Brookman ran Maud over?"

Salmone made a note to visit Jo Carr in counseling.

22

"I saw this coming."

Brookman stopped pacing and clenched his fists in pain.

"Please, sweetheart."

"No, I'm sorry, we have to live this out. I saw it."

"I ought not to be in this house at all," Brookman said.

"It's your house. And I'm your wife. Did you love her?"

"Did I love her?"

Can it be, he wondered, that I don't know what love is? But the fact was he had thought about it before. He had no answers, as was often the case. So he stood there in the room that had been contaminated for them by his treachery and tried to figure it out.

He had loved Maud as a woman, for her woman's body, as a person, for her human body. For her spirit, for her intelligence and courage. Person, body, intellect and will. He had even nourished a certain affection for her lack of judgment. Say it was for her youth and courage. She was not a child but in a way he had loved her as a child, as a daughter, a younger sister. He had loved her in all the ways that were supposed to be right and in ways that were wrong. He had not loved her in the all-consuming way in which he loved his wife or in the way he would love his children.

"No," he said.

"You did her great wrong," Ellie said. "I wonder what will happen to us now."

He said nothing.

"Let me tell you something strange," Ellie said to him.

He kept the liquor in a cabinet behind the piano in the quietly grand main room. For years he had resolved to move it somewhere else. Sophia practiced for hours every afternoon, and the sight of him hauling out a bottle of Dewar's past the pale small form of Sophia engaged in *The Well-Tempered Clavier* annoyed Ellie for reasons she herself could not have explained. Now, with Sophia safely in school, he fetched it out of the cabinet and poured himself a snifter.

"Tell me."

Her eyes took on the brightened gaze they sometimes held, a look Brookman secretly thought of as a glint of madness. "Glint of madness" because there were instances of what was apparently schizophrenia in her family, as there were many heritable diseases among the groups around White Lake.

"Last month while I was home, I first took the notion I was pregnant. I was almost sure. I was going to tell Mama. I was going to tell you."

They sat on a leather sofa, Ellie sliding to the far end from him.

"You didn't say anything," he said.

"Didn't want to jinx it. Anyway, I felt well. I thought I'd go along on a field trip over the mountains — across the Clears — with Nancy Gumm and two elders. We knew a norther was coming but I thought it was OK."

She meant the elders of her church, and Nancy Gumm was an ethnologist from Victoria. Brookman had not known. The storms were considerable this year.

"We were snowed in. Across the Clears. There are two families of our Christians there because years ago a madman brought their parents there. A man named Gross broke from the Old Synod. Think of Dürer. Think of Münster. They live with the Diné band there. There wasn't a winter road before drilling farther south. Old people remember before the money economy. Holiness Mennonites. Medieval. They live with the Carrier band there. The Diné. The native, the Indian band, the Carriers. No winter road.

"Nancy Gumm wanted to record. Because their songs are the oldest and the deepest in the north. And our folks who went and lived with them kept their songs going. And they sing and tell as though it were before Boas, that stupid man ... The Christian children do the same. They think in Carrier language, eh?"

She had been upset since the night of Maud's death but she seemed suddenly in the grip of something overwhelming.

"Did something bad happen there?"

She paid no attention to his question.

Ellie Brookman knew hundreds of Indian story-song performances. Teasing her, Brookman once told her it was like Comrade Zhdanov claiming to know two thousand Russian folktales, except that Ellie really knew the songs. Rarely did she talk about them with Brookman or anyone else. She might tell one narrative to him, or to people at a party, and she could make it funny, repulsive to the gentle ear, ironic.

But she knew people rolled their eyes heavenward if she so much as mentioned Indian tales. Once Brookman, flattering her, said, "You have a way with those stories, El. You get the point." This he intended as a joke. She would have told the stories in an absolutely white person's way, the humor and ironies and so forth completely changed for white people's perception. But she herself had learned to understand them in the intended native way. She would privately think: I won't be more of a fool than they think me now. Brookman and everyone else, she knew quite well, found the tales boring and pointless. Perverse at their most interesting, material for the many able parodists around.

Funny, she would think, how the despised Longfellow had done it best, using the rhythms of the *Kalevala*. It was all more different than people could imagine, and even she herself, until that winter, had not really known. But the mad Hutterite who took his pilgrims to the Clears had known.

"I would like to have some of your drink," Ellie told Brookman, "but I'm pregnant because you're so wonderful." She grinned and disappeared behind her eyes again.

"The midwinter time coming up, the midwinter ceremony. Darkness, darkness. Huge piles of birch, elder. Some they must have got at Bay Shopping Center a thousand miles away, hauled it in. Isn't that ironic, eh, but that's the life of the north, the bush. There are no ironies there. There's nothing but irony there. That's what the tales are all about. But the ceremony when the light goes, it will be gone for what, fifteen hours? The storm's trapped us and my thought is, I'm pregnant. I have to take care.

"Thank God Sophia was back at White Lake. Someone was singing a song about Coyote and I started to shake. Darkness all around. I thought I saw Coyote."

Ever so slightly she changed the angle of her strange, unfocused-seeming gaze and held him fixed.

"Coyote singing, 'Child will die, Elsa.' I thought: My land, we're fucked, eh? I thought we'll lose the child. But I didn't. No. Maud died instead. Ya. So I saw it coming."

Brookman finished his drink.

"Don't think I couldn't go into the bush and my cousins couldn't help me put up a cabin in a week," Ellie told him. "I could live there for the rest of my life. Never see you, never see anything but crows. Not man, woman, but stars and night and jack pine and I would still be your wife, do you understand?"

"Yes, baby," he said. "I understand." She was returning from the touch of transport, coming back to him.

"But I think I will not do that. And since you are here, you might do me the courtesy of staying."

"Every night of my life, Ellie."

"And days too, right? Mornings? Afternoons?"

"Day and night, Ellie. Yes, baby," he said. "I understand. But we're safe from that now."

"Yeah," she said. "I wish I could have a drink, but no way can I do that, right?"

"You're so right."

"Yes," she said. "You and me and God in heaven and the wonders of modern medicine can keep us pretty safe from that now. Don't do it to me again."

23

"I was very, very fond of maud," Jo Carr told Lieutenant Salmone. "I can tell you I'm in mourning for her. I was with her the night she died. For God's sake, find the person in that car."

He could see that she was very shaky but holding on. Holding on very well.

"You took her to the hospital, I understand."

"I took her to the hospital. I was told she left right away. I didn't try hard enough to find her. I let her wander off."

"Dr. Carr, you shouldn't feel that way, in my opinion. You did a lot more than your job."

"I let her wander off in a lot of ways."

"What could you do you didn't do?"

"Lieutenant, I like to think I can do a lot of things when I put my mind to it. You ask what I could have done? I don't know."

There was a box of tissues on the corner of her desk and he wondered whether she would make use of it herself.

"You know," she said, "I'd like to have a buck for every parent that ever came in here and said that to me. Myself, I never had any children of my own."

"I'm very sorry," Salmone said.

"Oh, it wasn't done, Lieutenant. I would have been the pregnant nun in the old joke — you get extra points for running her over."

"I meant I was sorry for your grief, Doctor."

"Right. Excuse me."

"Would you say Maud confided in you?"

"I couldn't exactly say that. For one thing, she wasn't terribly confiding. In her freshman year it might have been true."

"Not after that?"

"After that, hardly at all. But I believe I understood her. I felt I knew her well. Just intangibles. I know generally what's been up with her through other students affected by her life."

"You mean Shelby Magoffin?"

"Yes. You could talk to Shelby."

"We did. Anybody else?"

"Shelby, being her roommate, was the student closest to her I know about."

"She had a bad romance with Professor Brookman?"

"You might say that. Why are you asking me this?"

He told her about the scene on the street.

"They were shoving each other."

"Wait a minute, Lieutenant. Don't we suspect murder by an anti-abortion fanatic?"

"That's our leading possibility."

"What's it got to do with Professor Brookman?"

"We have to factor in everything."

Jo was silent for a moment.

"So she had a bad romance with Brookman. Understand this: Maud did not go in for romances. She was like the unobtainable girl and she broke their hearts. Some of them — in this place I think it was their first rejection. The boys, the alpha boys too, really went for her. And to speak for Brookman — as a married seducer — there were plenty worse. Or better at it. Or more compulsive. Maud was smart as could be. Beautiful, smart as could be . . ."

She stopped and looked at him. It was all he could do not to slide her the box of tissues. When she came around, he took one and wiped his glasses with it.

"Why are you asking me about Brookman?"

"I have to ask you, ma'am. So she thought maybe he would leave Mrs. Brookman?"

"I don't know about that. I know she thought it was love. Love love. She thought he adored her. He didn't talk about his family to her. She didn't know how married he was. How sort of devoted he was. She was quite young, she was self-absorbed. He's smart and attractive and traveled, and she thought he was hers."

"Permanently?"

"Oh," Jo said, "permanently? This was a kid. Forever and a day. Fairy tale. Vain. Aging, adoring parents. An A student here. Of course the mother passed away."

"Tell me about Brookman."

"They used to say about Brookman he was a polished thug. A very decent, likable guy in most ways. A boozy opportunist, not enough thought for the morrow, a very intelligent wife who loved him a whole lot and was from a stand-up-for-your-man tradition."

"Do you think he would hurt Maud?"

"No! Do you?"

"I don't know," Salmone said flatly.

"Frankly, I'd like to know why I'm being asked so much about him."

"Because of the way it happened. Why do you say Mr. Brookman is a thug?"

"That's entirely the wrong word," Jo said. "People used to say that as a joke."

"Yes?"

Suddenly she thought of El Doliente and her dream of him.

"It's funny," she said. "I should mention this priest I used to know in South America. He showed up here during the hassles that followed Maud's *Gazette* article. He came to see me. He's something of an anti-abortion crusader."

"He came here? To the counseling office?"

"He was called Father Walter. Down there we used noms de guerre. I mean we used just first names. Because it was dangerous."

Salmone wrote down what she gave him.

"Did he ask about Maud?"

"Yes. Everybody was all about poor Maud."

"Did he threaten her? Did he seem rational?"

"Frankly, I found him frightening."

"How so?"

"He was intense. I was frightened of him when I knew him years ago. He was a revolutionary. I guess I was too."

"South America this was?"

"Yeah. I think he might have been traveling with some Peruvian or Bolivian kids raising money."

"Father Walter," Salmone said. "We'll check him out. Did you say he threatened Maud?"

"No. But he asked about her. The night she died I had a dream about him. A very frightening dream."

"He scared you?"

"In the dream he did."

"We'll check him out if we can."

"I guess I was always scared of him," Jo said.

"Yeah, well," said Salmone, "some priests are like that. I think there were a lot of priests and ministers up here after that piece came out."

When Salmone was gone, Jo leaned on her desk looking down at its worn surface. Since when, she had to ask herself, do you use the cops as your friends and confidants? Not that she had anything against Salmone, whom she had encountered at least once before. The fixation on Brookman was puzzling and disturbing. She had spoken thoughtlessly and the detective's reaction was downright predatory. Were they going to scapegoat Brookman to cool the issue? No, she thought, surely that notion was just the ghost of her old activist conditioning. She hoped! But what had Brookman done? What had really happened? She had prattled on so thoughtlessly. It was taking place, and in a vacuum too, because the incident was so strange and shocking that partisan reaction was astonished and unformed. The week's *Gazette* had "ASK QUESTIONS!" on its front page as an editorial. Jo felt on her own with Maud's death.

She had already written and mailed a note of sympathy to Edward Stack. But since she had spoken with Stack the night of Maud's death, she decided to call him about arrangements.

He answered gruffly, as she expected. She reintroduced herself.

"I wondered how you were, Mr. Stack. If there was any way we could help?"

"They told me she's coming home," he said. "I want to put her with her mother."

"Yes. Well, look, would you please let us know about services? Anything that's not strictly family where we could say goodbye to her. People here loved and admired her."

"I heard."

Jo let that one pass.

"Some of us would like to . . . maybe say one for her. If there's a way. We'd like to remember her. Honor her."

"Yeah. I don't think she would want any church stuff. Just to be in the church where her mother is now. That would be it."

She waited for him to say more but he seemed to be finished.

"They told me she was coming home," he said again.

"I'll make sure of that, Mr. Stack."

"Hey, maybe I should make a contribution to you people. Maybe I should endow a girl's hockey stick. A lacrosse net."

"Mr. Stack," she said, "please stay in touch. Let us be here for you in any way we can. Do call me and let me know how you are."

She decided to call Lieutenant Salmone and ask about Maud's going home.

24

SALMONE HAD NOT HAD a call back from Eddie Stack, so he made another call of his own. He had thought a lot about it.

"I been thinking more and more we should sit down, Eddie. They must have told you this is a homicide one way or another. It may be involuntary, but it could be deliberate. Things I need to know."

"You don't have the driver?"

"We don't. You know how it is up here, the Staties doing that. They're checking out stops that night but, you know, it's incomplete."

"Yeah."

"She was drinking, Eddie. Kid drinking, you know? I'm really sorry — Maud and this Brookman, they were both drinking."

"I know about fucking Brookman. Brookman cut her loose. She was out of her mind."

"We're running down Brookman."

"The fuck is married. He's gotta be married, right?"

"Yeah, he's married. His wife is out there when it happens.

She's fucking pregnant. They're in front of his house. You heard that?"

"No. Not about the house. Sal? I gotta see you, man. I'll come up."

"If you could."

"You're working, Sal, I know that. I can do it."

"If you could, Eddie. It would be the best, I think, and soon, know what I mean? And us, we'll sit down quietly."

"Something I have to do first. I have to put Maud with her mother."

"That's good, Eddie. I'm so sorry. Call me and we'll talk."

25

AS JOHN CLAMMER DROVE THROUGH the deep woods, the sound of his sickly engine raised inquiring lights and groans in houses off the road. This was the accursed national forest famous for its tangled kudzu, its meth reek and the outlaw lives played out on the pulses of the strong, the failing and the weak among its inhabitants. No one had been meant to actually live there.

Of that place an arguably wise man once said: "This here is the Sherwood Forest. This here is the fucking Hole in the Wall where none but the strongest minds and wills fucking prevail in."

John drove to the Church of the Savior, where the U.S. government's road met the county highway, a neat assembly of metallic prefabs. There was a less neat double-wide positioned beside it where Dr. Russell Fumes, the church's pastor, lived with his young wife. The cleric's wife was not at home for John Clammer's visit, but Fumes himself was awake in bed, made uneasy by the sound of Clammer parking his vehicle.

"John!" the pastor exclaimed when his security lights caught Clammer about to knock on his door. "Lemme unlock it. I thought you was in the hospital, John. I thought your mother said you was under the weather."

As they sat by a lamp in the living room section, John explained himself. The lampshade had a deer-hunting scene printed on it: a hunter in an orange hat, his scope-enabled rifle, bright green trees, some sky. As far from the hunter as possible stood a twelve-point buck, an eastern deer, flag-tail up, poised to flee. The scene was made to fit two and a half times on the amount of plastic shade around the lamp.

"No, sir," John Clammer said. He told of how he had gone to the very so-called college his posturing wife had left him to attend. There he made an example of how the Lord would not be mocked with impunity. He had found the bitch who lived with his wife for evil writings.

"This!" he said. "Read it!" He trembled. He raised his fine eyes from the hunting scene on the lampshade and stared into the darkness under the artificial eaves. "For it is a screed! Yes, my good Reverend Fumes! A screed! But the little bitch is dead."

"You killed somebody, John? You didn't kill somebody."

John Clammer laughed and handed him a copy of a tabloid-size newspaper. The *Gazette*.

"Oh, yes! Oh, yes, my good doctor."

"Take it easy, John boy," Reverend Dr. Fumes said.

"She saw the glint of my rifle before I brought her down. And she fled me through the streets of that city screaming. She fled me. Down the nights and down the days!" John yelled, and it might have been a rebel yell or even a scream, as if in imitation of the young woman victim. "Down the labyrinthine ways!"

"Fuck sake," the preacher said, "take it easy." He put the newspaper aside. "What are you gonna do?"

"I'll turn myself in. I'll accept the penalties."

"Jesus, John, did you really do this?" Reverend Fumes looked away from the lamp and began to turn slow circles where he stood. "O Lord, my heart is troubled. My heart is blazing."

The reverend, a small man, was overwhelmed by John Clammer's presence and his declarations.

"I'll help you, John," he said. But how? He hoped that God might be seen as glorified in the events he was hearing about. He tried hard to find the workings of the divine will. He wondered if there was some way in which he himself could be seen as an instrument of glory.

Reverend Fumes sat back down beside the deer-hunting lamp and listened breathlessly while John Clammer told and retold the story of Maud's murder.

He presented the image of Maud clinging to his knees. After the echo of the last shot died, she had fallen at his feet in a posture of repentance. He had pitied her.

"I have forgiven the woman," John Clammer said. "That's what's most important."

John told Reverend Fumes he was in agony but would resolve it by accepting responsibility for his crime.

"Where's your rifle, John?" Dr. Fumes asked.

He said he had disposed of it in the forest. He said he invoked John Brown. He made Reverend Fumes swear to keep the secret of his blood guilt until he had presented himself to the police. He made the reverend bless him. As John Clammer poured forth his story, the reverend reflected more and more deeply on the role in which the Almighty had placed him. It might be that God had elected him to be the medium through which the work of his dread instrument John Clammer was made manifest to a chastened world. That the reading of the sacred dice cast behind the temple veil and enacted by this boy be announced from the Church of the Savior by its humble pastor. That it must fall to John to confess his blessed vengeance from within its precincts.

When John Clammer rose to go back to his pickup, Reverend Fumes blocked his path.

"Rest, John Clammer. We'll speak to the cops from the garden of Naboth while the dogs lick that bitch's blood."

He had hoped to please Clammer and persuade him that his wife or his wife's friend would be Jezebel. And there in the land where John Brown was being respected anew in a way not necessarily associated with people of color, there might be a singing of John's favorite hymn, "Blow Ye the Trumpet, Blow." Then Fumes would be Elijah-like and the church would be Naboth's vineyard and television's millions would bear witness and Fumes and the church would be exalted and theirs would be the kingdom and the power and the glory and the television exposure and the publicity and maybe the reality show. Michaiahjeroboamramethgileadsabaoth.

"Call from here, John. Surrender here in God's house. It'll be like . . ." Fumes thought about what it would be like. "It would be like sanctuary! Yeah! It would be like sanctuary. And they'd come out and like a hostage situation, Johnny!"

But John Clammer flung him aside like an old blanket and marched out the door and drove away toward town.

So Reverend Fumes had no choice but to get on the phone and call the sheriff's department.

"He confessed to me!" he shouted into the phone. "He's armed to the death on the county road! He confessed that evil woman's killing. He's armed to the teeth and headed for town."

26

STACK PUT OFF CALLING Salmone and the idea of going to the college. Attacks of dizziness kept striking him down, and in his grief, in despair, he felt older than he had ever been.

Then one day Salmone called him and said, "Eddie, I owe you the trip down. We still don't have the driver."

In another time and season they would have gone to Belmont or Shea from Stack's house. They had gone to those places on one or another of Salmone's visits years before, when Maud and her mother were alive.

Stack embraced his ex-partner and said there was nothing to drink; he was doing one day at a time. So they drank coffee, which agreed with neither of them terribly well.

Before they had talked very much Stack asked his dreadful question.

"You knew my brother-in-law?" Stack asked. "Charlie K.?"

"Yeah, yeah. I didn't know him. I heard about him years ago. I guess I knew he was your in-law."

"What did you hear about him, Sal? I have to ask this."

"Years ago, you know. Long time. Just who he was. Who he knew. Like his exploits."

"Listen. What I'm asking. Is there, was there — as far as you're aware — any possibility of malice against this family? Maybe Maud paid for a mistake."

"The mistake she made was fucking Brookman. The fucking guy Brookman, I mean. What do you mean, Charlie Kay?"

"His exploits in the thing happened downtown."

"You mean that —"

"Yes."

"I don't know what you mean, Eddie."

"Help that might have gone to Maud in college. Minuscule amount. Fucking minuscule. Through him as her uncle."

Salmone was silent. Studied him.

"Never," he told Stack. "Not a shadow. Not a whisper. Ever. Not that I would. I wouldn't have heard such a thing. Put it out of your mind, for Christ's sake."

Stack was burning in front of him.

"They'll get the driver, Eddie. They'll give it their attention. I will."

"I'm sorry. I'm fucked up."

"Look, tell me. What do you know about the relationship with Brookman? Was it violent?"

"I didn't ask her. I couldn't ask her. I wouldn't have asked that, Sal. Why?"

"Oh, there was a kid — a couple of kids, actually — thought they seen him push her."

Stack stared at him.

"I couldn't put that together," Salmone said. "Other people said they didn't see that. There's no case for that."

"No?"

"Won't stand up. But the guy did time."

"What the fuck?" Stack said.

"Yeah. It was . . . like it was technical. But the guy did federal time."

"What the fuck? The guy did federal time? This professor? He's what? He's some 'I was there' writer?"

"He's a big skinhead white guy. He was a fisherman."

Stack endured a moment's struggle for breath.

"Sal," he said when he had regained control of his voice. "You gotta run this down. This could be a very bad guy, brother. Placed where he is. He could hurt a lot of kids. It sounds like these students saw something. I mean . . . you gotta run this down."

"Eddie," Salmone said, "rest assured, man. If this fucking guy put a hand on her, he's going up. This is family to me. He's our number one person of interest as of this time. If there's more to find out, we're gonna find it out."

Salmone was thinking that he could hardly promise his

friend Brookman's head on a plate. Surely Eddie Stack must have a sense of how difficult, how nearly impossible, a conviction would be in the case as it seemed to stand.

"This guy," Stack said, "this Brookman . . ." He broke off to use his inhaler.

"What if he walks away from this, Sal? He's laughing. He's . . . laughing."

27

WHEN OFFICER BLANKENSHIP brought Salmone the bulletin from Boone announcing the apprehension of John Clammer, he immediately telephoned Shelby Magoffin's dorm room. When she answered, he asked her to stay where she was. He also called Polhemus, to do what he could to control the press hordes that he suspected might be making their way to the campus.

When Salmone got to Shelby's room, he was cross.

"Why didn't you tell us your husband was obsessed with Maud's piece in the *Gazette*?"

"'Cause he wasn't. He mentioned it but he wasn't bent out of shape or anything. The preacher down there must have been working on him. There's this dude named Dr. Fumes likes his name in the paper. He's been trying to work up a tabloid story about me and John."

"You didn't mention the protection order you had on him."

"Look, the protection wasn't even valid in this state. I put it in at the office here because I thought I might need it. I never thought he was a threat to Maud."

"Well, he's down in Kentucky confessing to Maud's murder."

Shell fell vertically on her sofa, landing on the seat of her pants.

"What?"

"The police down there are giving a press conference in half an hour."

"I don't believe it!" Shell said. "Hey, Lieutenant, John Clammer was either in jail or the hospital over that weekend. He never came around here. My mother checks up on him."

About half an hour later the cable news station announced the cancellation of John Clammer's press conference. He had been accounted for in custody on the night in question.

coat. There was a shorter man with him who was also watching Brookman pass. They were not each other's friends. They had no interest in their attractive surroundings or in the colorful characters who passed through the gate. Then it occurred to him that they were out-of-town policemen. He had seen at least one of them before but did not think it had been around the college. He passed people he knew, or who knew him, without recognition.

"You spent a lot of time at the office today," Ellie told him when he got home after six. She looked good, but not quite as radiant as she had been during the first pregnancy — a bit pale and more tired. Otherwise, she was not showing her condition.

There was one odd thing, which was they were having more sex. Brookman found this strangely, maybe perversely, satisfying. Ellie went about indicating her inclination silently, several times a week. When she came, which was more frequently than usual, she let him know it, moaning, breathless. Sometimes her face was wet as though with grief. She had always gone to sleep quickly but slept lightly. Listening for grizzlies, he had teased her in the days before Maud — alert to the wolf stalking the fold. Sometimes now, afterward, he told her that he loved her. She said nothing back, though she would often touch him. Her touches encouraged him but made him feel sad.

As he registered every remonstration of Ellie's, he watched Sophia with unsubtle caution for signs of resentment or withdrawal. Sophia watched him too, unconfiding, uncomfortable. She in turn was aware of his anxious observation. It was a delicate business to be conducted in such fearsome times, the guiding and nurturing of this wise, perceptive child at the cusp of adolescence. Sophia was both more and less sophisticated in certain ways than her contemporaries. Their bantering, fond relationship was a treasure of his life and he dreaded the loss of it.

During his hours in the office, he sometimes closed the curtains as he had when Maud visited. He ignored his e-mail and phone calls. Never answered his door. At times he drank, making sure that when he did, he had something to read. These were his two principal ways of controlling his guilt and grief. He had read Susanna Moodie's memoir *Roughing It in the Bush* in the federal detention center in Homer. It was a popular book among some of his homesteading friends in the old Alaska and he had a copy in his office. He did not get far rereading it. So he turned to work like Anthony Powell's. He read *The Quiet American* and Hemingway's *Men Without Women* along with a history of the siege of Berlin. Often he drank, keeping strong mints handy.

"People are looking at me strangely," he told his wife later that evening.

"Well, you're a strange guy, eh? Aren't you?"

Brookman went to check that Sophia was not in earshot. An afterthought. Then he went to pour himself a drink.

"Don't you think people look at me strangely?" she asked him.

"They suspect I pushed her."

Ellie failed to answer him at first.

"They once suspected you hit me," she said. "You took a swing at me."

"I've never hit you. And I never took a swing at you."

"Oh, ya. Years ago. The second time I ducked. You fight like my brothers. On one foot." After a moment she said, "Maybe they suspect me. Maybe they think we both hit her." Brookman laughed and shuddered.

"I didn't hit Maud, for Christ's sake. You were right behind me."

"Yes, I followed you out," Ellie said. He sat down on a kitchen chair, watching her in profile as she did the washing up. Her face was very handsome, not without faults. Her long, fine nose turned up slightly at the tip. While courting her, quite in love, he had discovered that she was a woman who believed, however humbly, that her course in life was directed by God and that her choices must be made to honor Him. Naturally, she did not always tell the whole truth but she was not a good liar. "I followed you out," she said truthfully. "Yes. The two of you."

"I didn't hit her," Brookman said.

"I might have," Ellie told him. "If she had turned toward my house."

A picture came to his mind, as vivid as though he had seen it, of snow falling past Maud's open blue eyes, flakes piling on their dead, still pupils. On her hair. At her throat. It did not incline him against Ellie. He had no clear idea how it made him feel.

"I'm going out."

"Taking the car? Bring in oatmeal." Ellie watched from the kitchen. Now she would not have the Christmas holiday she had been looking forward to — since being allowed a post-Mennonite Christmas — and her life was slowly changing from the inside out.

On the road Brookman drove with a defensive reticence that annoyed his fellow motorists. At the back of his mind was that some kind of unofficial police presence was on his trail. He had left the house without a destination.

29

Salmone had come to the house while Brookman was idly driving from one end of town to the other. Ellie had asked the detective to leave. Then she had telephoned him at the police station, gone in and made a brief statement describing what she had seen on the night of Maud's death.

"What did he say when you asked him to leave?"

"Well," Ellie said, "he didn't like it. He said he might have to ask me more formally for a statement later."

"Wonder what he meant by that."

While Brookman was sorting his thoughts, Salmone called and declared that he would like to come over.

"Shall I come in instead?" Brookman asked.

"Why don't you do that," Salmone said.

Brookman went out in the cold rain and walked to the police station. As soon as he saw Salmone's face he reflected on the interview Ellie must have provided. He was certain she had no idea how to favorably impress a sensitive, older, working-class detective.

He was right. Salmone was not happy with what Brookman's wife had told him. Obviously, the lieutenant thought, she had believed what she'd said. But her loyalty and composure, rendered with imperious reserve, did not make him like either Brookman any better.

"Have a seat, sir," Salmone said.

He let Brookman go through the details he recalled of the night in question without interrupting. He watched Brookman closely, letting him know he was being watched.

"Is it a fact, Professor, that you did time in a federal correctional institution?"

"I was a crewman on a crab boat. I was just out of the Marine Corps. Our boat was MV *Water Brothers,* out of Homer. We were over the limit on size and maturity. There were shoulder-seasonal changes I guess we weren't aware of."

"How come jail time?"

"We had a little petty grab-ass with the Coasties and I was up front. So I did three months in a converted prefab Air Force barracks outside Richardson. It was all fishery workers in there. They'd applied federal laws for years and then the state changed a lot of them."

"Too bad. You're a young kid practically. You were a veteran just out."

"Yeah. Sentences were way excessive. Everyone says that."

"Tough. But you did OK in later life. Here you are . . ."

"Yeah." Brookman had the sense that Salmone was speaking to him more as an apprehended perpetrator than a college professor.

"Very sad about this young lady. Do you have some more to tell us?"

"How would I?"

"I don't know, Mr. Brookman. Maud Stack comes to your house. It's a blizzard outside. She's troubled and intoxicated. But you don't let her in. Why?"

Brookman looked at him a while before he answered.

"She was there to intimidate me. And my family."

"Really?"

"That's right."

"You didn't think you could help her?"

"Only by suggesting she leave."

"You figured you could help her by suggesting she leave?"

"Yes."

"Did you shove her out?"

"Shove her? Of course not."

"Guide her back in the street?"

"I didn't touch her."

"I'm sorry, Mr. Brookman. We have cell phone videos. You're touching her. You're actively touching her."

"When we were in the street and the traffic was coming I tried to pull her back on the sidewalk. That's what you have a record of."

"Myself, I'm surprised you forced her out on the street in the weather."

"I didn't force her out on the street. I told her to go home. If she'd done what I told her, she'd have been all right."

"But you lost your temper?"

"I didn't lose my temper, Lieutenant Salmone. I did not lose my temper. I asked Miss Stack to go back to her dorm because I have a child in the house who I thought might be frightened."

"You could have called us."

"There was no need."

"Maybe there was. Maybe she oughta have called us."

"Nobody needed the police then. It was personal. It was not violent. We didn't require cops."

"Maybe it was a lovers' quarrel, huh? Because everybody in this place knows you were in bed with this girl. Sounds like she was in your way big-time. Maybe she should have called us."

"Are you accusing me of pushing her in front of a car?"

"What if I tell you I have people saw you do that?"

"You can't, goddamn it! What people saw was me trying to get her out from in front of the traffic! Both our lives were in danger." He rose from his chair. Salmone backed his own chair away. "What bullshit are you people trying to sell? Is this the college you're working for or what?"

"It's against the law to sleep with your student."

"It is not against the fucking law, Salmone! Adult-on-adult sexuality is not illegal. As yet."

"It's against the college rules."

"That's not your problem, sir!"

They glared at each other across the desk.

"Hard-ass," Salmone said. "Aren't you, Professor?"

"Too hard for you, Mr. Cop. If you try to make some kind of killer fiend out of me, I swear I'll sue you, your city and anybody who I catch collaborating with you in such a scheme."

Brookman settled in his seat and put his elbows on the desk. There were a few other city cops working in the station and they stopped to listen. A few of them moved closer to Salmone's office.

"Maybe I should have driven her home," Brookman said. "Obviously I should have driven her home."

Salmone said nothing.

"Are we finished?" Brookman asked.

Salmone stood up.

"Who do you think that driver was?"

Brookman stared at him in surprise.

"I hope you find him."

"We always do," Salmone said. "You have anything more to tell us, Professor, you have my card. Don't hesitate. You gonna be around?"

Brookman thought about it for a moment. His not being around was an idea that had not occurred to him.

"Well," Salmone said. "We'll be here."

Brookman decided to engage a lawyer the next morning.

30

ONE COLD DAY STACK TOOK the Long Island Rail Road to the McCallum and Jenkins funeral home, the people who had contained his wife's ashes.

"I'd like my daughter's remains beside my late wife's," he told the slightly overweight, fair-haired undertaker, a McCallum. McCallum expressed his sympathy, especially for a person so young. Stack saw that his sympathy was as genuine as it could be in such circumstances. The younger McCallums went to seminars and did meditation to the tinkling of bells.

"Have you arranged this with the church, sir? I presume interment will follow a Mass of resurrection."

"I don't think she would want a Mass."

"Mr. Stack, isn't your late wife at the cathedral?"

"Holy Redeemer, right."

"It would follow the same procedure, Mr. Stack. May I ask why you believe Ms. Stack wouldn't want a Mass?"

"She wasn't religious. She loved her mother very much. She

missed her mother a whole lot. She would want to be beside her."

"Sir," the young man said gently, "it all goes together. Can you be sure she wouldn't want to follow mom's way?"

"I have no beef with you," Stack explained. "I'm hoping to take care of this."

"We'll follow your instructions, Mr. Stack. I think we've served the Stack family for generations."

"Since your place was on First Avenue."

It was true, although Stack had never much thought about it. McCallum and Jenkins funeral parlors had managed to remain local, moving in the same pattern of families like the Stacks, from certain Manhattan neighborhoods. They had buried a lot of soldiers since after the Civil War. Different kinds of people favored different firms, and M&J was well regarded by the unlucky. The McCallums had extended credit to prisoners' widows without benefits or influence, and for reasons of their own they had served AIDS victims from the beginning. There were those who disliked that.

"One thing we can't do," McCallum said, "is guarantee a place with Ms. Stack's mother in Holy Redeemer. They have their rules and costs, et cetera. So you'll have to deal with them, Mr. Stack."

"The urns are standard, right?"

"Sir?"

"The urns, the whaddaya calls? What you put ashes in. They all look alike, right? Do you make them? Do you sell them?"

"Usually . . . ," McCallum said.

"Pick up my Maud. Put her in the thing. I'll talk to the church then. I need to do this, see."

He gave McCallum a copy of the death certificate.

"It's a very simple ceremony," McCallum said. "These physical things, the earthbound things, they're partly for friends and family. In the tradition."

"Still," Stack said. It was what Maud would have said.

"I don't know what to say, Mr. Stack. I'm sorry."

"I'm determined to try to get Maud what she wanted. She never had a life."

McCallum looked him in the eye.

"I can understand your feeling that, Mr. Stack. The thing is, we've always worked with the church. Within its traditions."

"I'll talk to them. I want my daughter with her mother."

"We can do a lot of things to serve you, Mr. Stack. I can't simply get your daughter's remains into Holy Redeemer Church."

The next day he took the train to the cathedral to look at the niches along the wall. Ashes were held in little marble-like repositories that had lids on the tops like cigarette boxes, and in glass cases like imitation medieval reliquaries Stack remembered growing up with. In his own parish church in Richmond Hill there was a bone in a similar case. The faithful would kneel devoutly in front of the bone and smooch the glass on the front of it so that there was always a surface of spittle-laced, fogged-up glass on the case containing the alleged bone of Saint Wallbanger or something reposed in it. Next to it was a gray rag of dingy sheeting to wipe the glass with, in order not to catch polio or mouth fungus or something like it from the glass. Sane people who felt compelled to take part in this kissy game staged a lip-smacking air kiss and pumped the rag on the front of it, wondering what diseases you could catch off the cloth. It was a disgusting little sacramental moment a guy could joke about with the right people.

ironize or shave inflections in times of trouble. "John will be in in just a moment. You don't need anything?"

He listened to her withdrawing heels on the polished hall-way floor and was actually comforted.

The dean received guests in the sort of elegant room that went with his job. As he sat in it, waiting, Brookman medi-tated on the footsteps of the woman who had addressed him, a woman he liked and admired, a woman much observed and speculated upon at the college.

She was a very attractive blue-eyed brunette, English in congenial and unthreatening ways. As had become virtually required, she had an occupation in addition to being the dean's wife; with a certificate in art history from the Courtauld, she held a position at an auction house that took her twice a week to New York. This allowed some college folk to refer to her as a gallery strumpet. Because she was so fine and reticent she had become the object of fantasies. People, particularly people who disliked John Spofford, hoped she had a lover, likely in New York. Egotists, mostly male, dreamed. Mrs. Spofford was used to lingering glances — even to the rare boozy attack of footsie — at dinner parties. She coped without effort. In their dorms, her student admirers waggled and blazed. What secrets had she?

One of her secrets was that every Sunday she walked a mile and a half, in every weather, in an ankle-length raincoat and with a scarf tied under her chin, to St. Blaise's, a ruinous church where a Mass was said at eight in the morning in Latin by a tiny, eighty-something Irish priest. Occasionally she helped an elderly Ecuadorian cleaning woman tidy the retired priest's back-garden apartment. Both the priest and the old lady would stand at some sort of attention when Mrs. Spofford arrived, and she had given up trying to put them at ease. Once the priest had started to rise from his chair at her presence, and she had discouraged his doing it so commandingly that he had almost died sitting there. Mrs. Spofford was sometimes useful at Mass because he often forgot the responses and she had them handy.

Dean Spofford looked up from the pile of college-printed documents he had been signing. Handouts. Condolences. The kinds of palliative statements he was so good at. He stared at Brookman.

"I know what you're going through," the dean said, touching Brookman's knee. "I know that sounds stupid," he added.

Brookman, humiliated at the sound of the words, closed his eyes and shook his head.

The dean straightened himself in his chair. "Sorry, Steve. Really."

"It's all right, man. What is there to say? It's hard to imagine."

For a moment Brookman thought he might really go to pieces, cry on the bastard's shoulder. A practiced shoulder, no doubt, often cried on by innocence, misfortune, bereavement, remorse. It made him, on second consideration, regret that Mary Spofford had espied him there. He liked and admired her so much and dreaded what she must have been thinking. For a moment he silently observed the dean's discomfort. Would he let me cry on his wife's shoulder? He would have loved to cry there.

"So I've spent the last forty-eight hours wondering what our reaction should be," Spofford said.

There were limits. Brookman brought himself under control.

"Whose reaction? Reaction to what? To my killing Maud Stack?"

"Nobody thinks you killed Maud Stack, Steve, but I can tell you what they do think. They think you encouraged and seduced her, taking advantage of your age, experience and position at the college. Abused your responsibility to her and your duty as her professor."

"Give me a break. You never slept with a student? You didn't know about me and Maud Stack? You don't know, as we speak, about other liaisons in this place?"

"Caused in her as a result of that exploitation an emotional state that led to her involvement in a fatal accident. And that your encouragement and seduction was widely known in spite of your being a parent in this community and long married to our friend and colleague Ellie. And people think that those in a position to intervene, to say a word, lay a hand on your cuff and advise you — nay, tell you — to cut it out, did nothing. Knew and did nothing. That's what people think."

Brookman said nothing.

"Your request for a leave is denied. Nor will your contract be renewed. As for your questions: I have never slept with one of my students. I emphasize that this speaks only for my discretion. I did know about you and the late Maud Stack. I know about the liaisons of which you speak. I know and the trustees know and even His Dimness the President knows, and I'm going to pay for it. He's going to pay for it too."

"Sorry," Brookman said.

"It's all right, Steve. I should have seen it coming. It's an age of transition, isn't it? The old arrangements fall before the new arrangements. That which was unspeakable may thrive and is blessed. That which was tolerated is an abomination. We've been living it. The fine old shit don't float. Now me — I'll never get a billet like this — that I enjoy so much — again."

The front door opened and closed, and the dean looked through the curtained window to see his wife greeting two young women on the street outside.

"Will they really sack you, John? Over this?"

"Yeah. Not just this, I suppose. But yes, they really will."

"I really am sorry," Brookman said.

"Sure. But enough about me — let's talk about you. You have a month to quietly vacate. If you want to haggle over details, get a lawyer."

Brookman started to stand up.

"Hear me out. Will Ellie leave if you do? Because naturally she can stay, no problem."

"I'm pretty sure she'll go with me. I hope she does."

"Too bad, because it's unlikely she'll find a setup like this anytime soon either. I'll do what I can to see that the college gives her all the recommendations she needs. People may not be as helpful to you because they see you as an outdoors writer. Rather than an educator."

"Yes," Brookman said. It was awful about Spofford and even more awful about Mary Pick because of the horrors that had occurred in her life and the comfort she had found at the college. He appreciated Spofford's not mentioning it. It was all he could do not to apologize again.

On his way to the department office to give notice that he would not be conducting his class next semester, he passed her, chatting with her two companions. He felt as if there on the street he might actually lose his composure.

32

AFTER THE WEEKEND Stack decided it was time to lay Maud beside her mother. Another spell of warm winter weather had settled on the region. Monday was the warmest December day in seventy years. He took the train out to Nassau County, to the Church of the Holy Redeemer, where his wife's ashes reposed. He had left a voicemail message with McCallum and Jenkins the day before, letting them know about his intention. He called McCallum again before setting out and this time reached the man himself.

"We may have run into a snag," McCallum said.

"What snag? You have everything ready, don't you?"

"We have everything ready on our side. I expected to hear from the bishop's office, but judging from their call today I don't know if they've made a decision."

"I want to do this today. If I don't get it done . . ." He left the statement unfinished. "I want to get it done."

"I'd wait until we heard from them."

"Are you in today?"

"Yeah, I'm in," McCallum said. "But I'd wait."

"I'll be over," Stack told him.

He took a taxi from the station to the funeral parlor. At the front entrance he found he had to ring for admittance. There was no one inside except James McCallum, funereally dapper, at his desk in the front office. The lingering scent of lilies, he supposed, must be constant. He sat down in one of the chairs intended for mourning clients and took out his checkbook. The undertaker had an itemized bill ready for him, and Stack wrote the check for the full amount.

"So," Stack said, "do we take it over?"

"Well, the thing is," McCallum said, "I haven't got their consent quite yet."

"Fuck their consent."

"I don't know if that's the attitude. Look," he said before Stack could answer, "let me show you."

When he came back he had a rectangular box that looked as though it might be made of slate. It was slate-colored, very dark gray and marked with a dark green cross like the ones that illuminated medieval Celtic manuscripts.

"You didn't tell us, Mr. Stack. We had to hope it was satisfactory."

"You mean it's done?"

"That was how we interpreted your instructions. We had to take the risk it would be all right."

McCallum held the box toward him in a way that presented him with the option of taking it or not.

Stack put his hands out stiffly and took hold of it. It was cool and smooth, considerably bigger and heavier than he had expected. McCallum rose and quickly took it from him and laid it in front of a gray curtain behind his desk.

"I very much hope it's all right. Mrs. McCallum and I . . ."

"It'll be fine," Stack said. He had resolved to make them put Maud with Barbara.

"You look angry."

"I'm not angry at you."

He was surprised to hear mention of Mrs. McCallum because he had taken James McCallum for gay. In fact, the Mrs. McCallum referred to was McCallum's mother.

"So I should take it now," Stack said. "Let's take it over."

"Well, they haven't made the call. I talked to them and I thought I had arranged it but they haven't made the call."

"That's OK," Stack said. "We'll just take it there."

"What if they don't accept it?"

"Don't accept it? What do you mean?"

"Well," McCallum said in some confusion. "I was talking to a friend over there. I thought it would be all right. Now it's unclear."

"I'll go clear it up."

"I don't know," McCallum said.

"Give me the . . . thing there. What do you call it?"

"Casket. It's a casket."

Stack went and got it.

"I thought it was 'cremains' or some shit."

"Mr. Stack, please."

"Casket. I'm going to take it over there to the church."

McCallum rose from his chair and stared at Eddie Stack.

"I'd better go too."

"Why?" Stack demanded, gripping the box. "What do you mean, you better go too?"

"Believe me, Mr. Stack. I should go. There are laws. If for some reason they don't take it — I mean, I really thought they would — there are laws about transporting remains in New York State. You have to have a license."

Stack and McCallum drove over to Holy Redeemer in McCallum and Jenkins's Lincoln Town Car.

"I was thinking," McCallum said as they drove. "You seem angry. So I'm thinking of the laws."

"I appreciate it," Stack said. "Does this cost me more?"

Maud's remains were strapped into the rear seat.

"Are you serious? Of course not."

On the way, McCallum kept trying to call his friend or whoever it was at Holy Redeemer who had encouraged his optimism, but he failed to make contact. When they got to the cathedral the undertaker parked in the space reserved for funerals.

"Nothing today," he told Stack. "Except us.

"We'll go to the rectory," McCallum said. Stack, carrying the casket, kept falling behind, out of breath. Then McCallum changed his mind. "No, we won't. We'll go to the crypt — we'll ring for the sexton." So they reversed course and headed for the church itself.

Holy Redeemer had been built in the mid-1970s. It was a long, vaulted building with two huge winged structures on either side, like the flying buttresses on a Gothic cathedral. Both of the buttresses were larger than the vaulted construction in the center. They climbed three low, expansive steps and found every door of the main building's entrance locked. McCallum went over to a small brass disk beside one door, a doorbell of sorts. It looked like a very old device, something from another era. Stack thought it might have come from an older church and been rigged up for this one. Above it was a plaque that read "Ring Bell for Sexton." McCallum pressed it. No sound was audible where they stood. Stack heard no result. He set the casket down and wiped the perspiration from his brow.

"So warm today," McCallum said to Stack. "Don't worry," he added. "This'll work." He seemed to have grown optimistic.

"Good," said Stack.

Somewhat to Stack's surprise, after a few minutes the door with the ring button beside it opened and a man in a black cassock came out and looked at them in a not particularly welcoming manner. He was wearing a civilian collar with a red tie under his cassock and seemed to be some kind of layperson, presumably a sexton. Stack recalled hearing or encountering the term "sexton," but its meaning was unclear to him.

The man's gaze immediately fell on the casket with Maud's ashes in it. Stack found his stare somewhat offensive. He seemed to know McCallum and to not much care for him.

"What are you two doing here with that, McCallum?"

"This is Detective Stack," McCallum said. "Detective, this is Arthur Porgest, the assistant sexton here."

A detective was a good thing to be in Arthur Porgest's world. He shook Stack's hand.

"Mr. Stack unfortunately suffered the loss of his daughter. He wanted to place her remains alongside her mother's. I'm sure it would be all right."

"You'll have to ask the monsignor."

"No, no," McCallum said. "We can unlock the crypt and put her up there."

"I can't just do that," said the sexton.

"Sure you can," Stack said. "Just do it."

Porgest stalked off, leaving them on the steps, and came back with a pale, slight, bald priest with a purple band framing his Roman collar. The priest had a pamphlet in his hand. He raised it to his forehead to shield his eyes from the bright winter sunlight, the better to see them more clearly.

"Hello, Mr. McCallum," he said. "Let me guess. Would this be Mr. Stack?"

"I'm Eddie Stack," Stack said. "I've brought my daughter here. I mean, I've brought her body here."

McCallum and the priest looked down at the white steps of the church, away from the casket.

"We've heard about your need from Mr. McCallum. I'm Father Washington." He put his hand out but Stack did not take it. "I'm afraid this is still under discussion."

"What do you mean, 'this'? Letting my daughter be with her mother? I want to put her here now."

"This is embarrassing," the priest said.

"Is it?" Stack asked him.

The priest, smaller by several inches than McCallum or Stack, kept the pamphlet at his forehead and looked at them with what seemed great intensity. Because of his baldness and the smoothness of his head, the reflected glow he cast was impressive.

"For one thing, I'm afraid I can't ask you into the rectory at the moment. Or ..." He gestured beyond the tall doors of the church. "We may not look busy today, but we are. His Eminence hasn't made a decision on this."

"Couldn't we," McCallum asked, "just place Miss Stack's remains now? And perhaps talk later."

"Mr. McCallum," the priest said, "we are not a convenience-store operation. You don't drop in on us. You," he told McCallum, "of all people, should know that. And," he told Stack, "you should too, sir."

"Mr. Stack is a police officer," McCallum told the priest.

"Is that right?" Father Washington asked. "Very fine. Thank you for your service. Actually, I think I read that somewhere."

"How about opening up and receiving the kid's ashes?"

"Yeah, well," Father Washington said in a strange tone, different from the brisk one he had been employing. "Now you want us."

"Yeah," Stack said. "Now I want yez."

"Not so easy," said the priest, with the hint of a smile.

"I think she wants her mother. I think her mother wants her there."

"I'm sorry," Father Washington said softly. "I haven't the authority."

"She made a mistake," Stack said. "I guess you heard about that. But she wants to be with her mother. Her mother would want that."

The priest looked at each of them in turn with renewed energy. "Look here, guys. Let's put Maud away for the weekend and we'll all discuss it further. His Eminence—"

"Put who away?" Stack asked him, biting his lip. "Who we putting away?"

McCallum put a hand to Stack's arm.

"Why, the young lady," Father Washington said. "I mean . . . Miss Stack's remains." He took a half step back toward the door.

"Let's put them with her mother, Father," Stack said.

"Look, McCallum," said the priest. "When you get back to the funeral home you can explain this to him."

"You explain it," Stack said to the priest. "You explain it to me."

Father Washington turned away and disappeared through the church door that was unlocked. Porgest, the sexton, had been standing just inside.

As they drove back—Maud strapped in the back seat again— McCallum started to explain.

"It's a very conservative diocese, Mr. Stack. Other places would be more flexible. They'd be — I hope they'd be more understanding."

"That's OK," Stack said. "Not your fault."

They placed Maud's ashes in a curtained room behind the funeral home's office.

"You weren't drinking today, were you, Mr. Stack?"

"Not for the last two days. I'm still buzzing, though. Still intoxicated."

"I'm sure they'll see their way clear. They're a very stuffy bunch here. And Washington, he's a difficult man."

"Have you been drinking, Mr. McCallum?"

McCallum smiled and wiped his brow again.

"Not for eleven years," he said.

33

JO NEVER HEARD FROM Edward Stack about whatever arrangement he had made for Maud's interment with her mother. When she checked with Lieutenant Salmone, she learned that Maud's remains had been sent to New York. However, Salmone told her, the church in Nassau County was making difficulties. And there was no further word on the car or the driver.

After thinking about it Jo decided to call Dean Spofford's wife, Mary Pick, at her New York auction house. Mary said she would stop in on the way home.

From her nearly sidewalk-level corner window Jo saw Mary Pick's hired car swing around the square and stop in front of the one-way sign at the end of Jo's block. She watched the rain spot the tops of Mary's shapely Cole-Haan shoes as the dean's lady came briskly to the counseling center's door.

Jo and Mary had each soldiered through the unraveling ranks of the Catholic religion on various of its forced marches through the abysmal sleep of reason. They had both borne the guidon

Credo quia absurdum. Mary, bred in the bone, had proved the stauncher trooper, with a commando's grip on *absurdum.* Jo had taken a deep breath and bailed, and felt just fine on her own two feet. Nevertheless they had become acquainted through Jo's contacts with members of the Newman Club, which had once included Maud Stack. What they had been compelled to know, believe and not believe, served to make them close friends at the college. Even to the point that Jo had accompanied Mary on a few of her dawn patrols to St. Blaise's, strictly as an observer. She could risk being seen in that company. Jo also knew things many did not about her friend.

Mary Pick's first husband had been blown in half, and her son almost completely blinded, by an IRA bomb placed under an ice cream vendor's truck in Belfast on a May Day afternoon. Thereafter it was never pointed out in her hearing that Captain Pick had been present as a British official in Ireland attendant on government service. As it happened, Picks had been Catholics since the Conqueror, and had chosen to surrender their estates and preferments at the Reformation to remain so for the next four hundred years. Mary Pick had taken her cranky blinded eleven-year-old boy for an endless train ride down France to Lourdes, in the course of which she had been subjected to many tearful questions. Lourdes had not provided the hoped-for intercession, so there was the desolate ride back. Now Mary Pick was at the college, married to the agnostic, rather saturnine John Spofford. Her son, tall and possessed of his father's mili-tary bearing, was now a Labour member of Parliament distinguished by the white-painted, leather-handled shepherd's crook he used as a guide stick, a small joke of his own. He was married to a famous London journalist not warmly loved by Mary Pick.

Jo told Mary about the contretemps with the church on Long Island.

"We should profane the service of the dead," Mary Pick recited.

Jo, startled a moment, understood that she was quoting *Hamlet*.

"Surely they don't keep that kind of score, Mary."

"The priests have become very arrogant. Again."

"Their cause seems to be prospering in spite of every revelation," she told Mary. "If you don't mind my saying so."

"Their cause? I don't know what cause they serve, some of these men."

Jo got up from the desk and turned on the room's overhead fluorescent lights. One of them nursed an irritating hum. She looked out at the puddles in the street through the wire mesh that encased the windows. The mesh dated from the days when the old building was a city school to be protected from errant fly balls.

"I'm concerned for the father," Jo said, keeping an eye on the rain. "He's elderly and now he's alone. A widower. Retired policeman. No other kids. A bitter, bitter man. Drinks. He's lost to the living world soon."

"Did he know she'd had an abortion?"

"She never did have one. That's what she told me, and I certainly believed her."

"Funny," said Mary.

"You could kind of tell it in the piece she wrote. That it was by someone outside the process."

"How strange," Mary said. "I thought that as well." She smiled faintly. "I thought, What a vain creature. How little she knows."

"I understand the bishop down on Long Island doesn't want to put Maud's ashes in the crypt — in the niche, whatever — with her mother. It would just be a favor, a neat thing to do. But he wants her father to commission a formal Mass of interment. In other words, come crawling and they'll take her home."

They sat on the table at opposite ends under the ugly whining light.

"Oh, the bishop's an old skunk, isn't he?" Mary said. "Wants her father to remember his daughter as a pagan and a sinner and a disgrace to her mother. With whom she will never be reunited. But he can't pretend to cut a Christian soul off from her salvation. Over a piece written by an adolescent in a college newspaper."

"He's probably incapable of thinking it through that far, Mary. Who knows what he believes? Who knows who he is? What kind of people become bishops anymore?"

Jo got up and switched off the ceiling light, to kill its glare and turn off its noise.

"Quite all right," Mary said, "some of them."

"Really? If you say so. But you're a very tolerant person."

"Oh, dear," said Mary Pick. "I've never been told that before."

Jo sat and watched her elegant friend.

"I want to ask you something. I have to ask it. But I'm afraid you won't be my friend anymore after I do."

"Oh, my," Mary said. "Let's see."

"How can you align yourself — a person like you — how can you ally yourself with such terrorizing by such people?"

"I can't, because I don't. I am not an activist or an agitator. I can only tell you why I couldn't have had an abortion. Why I think people shouldn't do it. But you'll know all about that."

"Yes."

"If anyone asks me," Mary said, "I'll say don't do it. There are people who don't believe human life starts at conception. I can't prove them wrong. We are taught that the universe is beautiful. We believe it is good. We believe its phenomena reflect a perfection beyond our understanding but that we can partly experience. Sort of. Man — I should say humankind, shouldn't I? — is also sacred. Reflecting that being we know as God. Matter, stuff, quickened to human life, is therefore sacred. At the moment, we are taught this quickening happens on conception."

"At the moment."

"We don't argue, do we, because this is dogma, isn't it?" Mary said. "That is the inspired teaching at the present time. Faith. A being sacred in that way is not to be destroyed at will. Cannot be judged worthy of destruction for individual or general human advantage. That's the Church's teaching and that's the faith one practices."

"And everyone else has to practice it too?"

"I hold sacred what is declared sacred. The law of the state cannot justify abortion. It isn't the law of the state that makes human life sacred. It can't determine what is mortal sin or blasphemy. It can't punish spiritual crimes. It can't presume to speak for God."

"I never thought you felt any other way, Mary."

Mary looked at her watch. "Got to make dinner for Deano. Ask me if he hates being called Deano. Plucked it from an inspired moment."

"Wish I'd been there."

"Right," said Mary Pick. "You're never there. No one's ever there when I'm inspired."

Jo walked to the door and they looked through the glass at the rain. Mary borrowed an umbrella from Jo's enormous stash of forgotten ones.

"Not to worry, Josephine," Mary Pick said, her hand on the knob. "We'll get things put right for Maud's father. The church . . . thing."

"Hey, Mary? Did you think Maud's piece was good? Religion aside, sort of?"

"Religion aside? A writer lost to us there. I'm going to pray for her. I like to pray that all will be well in spite of things. You know, 'All shall be well, and all shall be well, and all manner of thing shall be well.' In spite of it all. You should try it, really. Why not?"

"I'll leave it to you. I'm glad you liked her piece."

"I didn't say I liked it."

"But you thought it was good."

"Oh, yes! Time loves language, you know. Forgives the writer, the poet says. And here we are." She gestured in the direction of the college's well-known library. "Books everywhere. We do too."

34

ACCORDING TO THE afternoon timetable, Stack had to change trains at what had been a derelict station in Connecticut he had not seen in a few years. His last time through it had been a crack scene, a rat-haunted vault of pissy shadows. It had been improved somewhat since the downtown bombings. Maybe, he thought, one thing had to do with the other. Graffiti had been painted over. The fluorescent lights in the ceiling were as yet unvandalized, but the ticket counter was closed and the only person in the station with him was a suspiciously sleepy teenager in a hoodie. Stack went over and looked at him — a police impulse. The boy's eyes were half closed. The kid never reacted, and it was as though he were trying to hide in plain sight.

Stack, in his best wool pants and rather shabby sport jacket, walked tilted against the weight of the semi-automatic pistol he had taken to carrying. New York cops had been issued Glocks while Stack was in the job. Glocks, which replaced the old revolvers, were fearsome, fateful pieces, and they could set a running man into an airborne spin. It was a weapon to display on a twenty-first-century coat of arms, Stack thought. If there was a piece of weaponry used to claim the streets, it would be the Glock, exploding into random fusillades. A carelessly drawn breath might set it blazing. A gun with a mind of its own, in the world that had come to be after 9/11 — heavy, hard to use, ready to take out half the room in seconds. They had become popular. Prestigious weapons, they tempted bozos toward casual display.

The Glock had led to a pandemic of bizarre shootings. Things happened inexplicably, the gun creating absurd occurrences on the streets. He had not packed it since leaving the job, and it felt strange.

On the next train to the college Stack had his choice of seats. At New Haven he rose to change again and walked across the refurbished station's interior. By Maud's time they had cleaned it up, as befitted the classy young passengers who used it. Of whom Maud had been one. From New Haven a slow local train tunneled through the hills and up the river to Amesbury.

35

JO WAS IN THE OFFICE, closing it down for the holiday break. Amid the spreading tremors of accusation and fear that attended Maud's death, she'd been giving the semblance of advice to students preparing to return transformed to their families. The home folks would be welcoming conditions as various as bird flu, drug addiction, kundalini yoga, and Salafism, and offering returnees a few unexpected variations on the lives they'd left behind. In short, it was a tough time anyway, compounding the elements of Christmas, the kids' ages and so on. Mercifully for the college, the repercussions, for the most part, didn't have to be acted out on college property.

Jo was almost finished with the mailings when an old man came through the street door upstairs and descended to her office.

"Miss Carr?" the old man asked. Jo smiled. "I'm Eddie Stack. I used to be Maud's father."

His way of putting it cut off her polite greeting.

"You'll always be her father, Mr. Stack. Through eternity."

"We talked on the phone," Stack said. "You and me. The night before she died."

She told him to sit down and took a place opposite him.

"I took her to the hospital that night because she was so upset. But she got away from me. You mustn't say you used to be her father, Mr. Stack."

She rose and shook his hand across the desk.

"Whatever you say," he told her.

"I've told you how desolate we've been here. It makes such an awful Christmas."

"Yeah," Stack said. "It's too bad. I see they got the streets in town decorated. I came up from Long Island."

"We miss her so much," Jo said. Stack was trembling a little. She wondered whether he had been drinking, and for how long.

"I know they liked her here. I heard."

She could only take it for bitterness, and what could she say? That Maud was admired and loved here in ways with which she could not cope, before her time. That Maud herself had loved it here, that it was the fullness of life to her. That it almost certainly would have been fine in the end with a little luck and a little less of God's appalling mercy.

"But you got her now, right?" Stack said. "You got her from me."

She looked into the man's ruined, unforgiving face. We lost you your pretty one. Forgive us!

"Mr. Stack," she said. "I was going to call you today. You

spoke about putting Maud with her mother? I understand that the church is making ... difficulties?"

Stack writhed in his chair, and the scornful smile he gave her made her cringe as if she herself were the Church and the college and the self-indulgent faculty, all proclaiming their false love, their greed, their treachery.

"Well, look, Mr. Stack. One of our folks here is very active in the Church. And she's arranged an interment for Maud with her mother at the earliest convenient time. And there'll be a priest. A ceremony, if you require."

"So you people," Stack said, "you people up here, you can do anything, right?"

"No, sir," Jo said. "We can't. But we are people who care. Many of us."

Stack sat silently for a moment, not looking at Jo. Then he stood up, walked to the window and watched the people above him in the street. A few students remained around the campus, selling their textbooks at the only independent store left in town, buying souvenirs for their friends and family.

"I don't want a religious ceremony," Stack said. "The priests can shove it. I want to put the kid with her mother."

"We'll do it, Mr. Stack. This week. In Advent."

"I heard about this youth down south said he killed Maud," Stack said.

"That was a false confession. A nutcase."

"Yeah, I know. What about this Brookman? Some people say

he pushed her in front of the car. The professor who seduced her. The ex-con."

"No, sir. Can I call you Ed? It was another crazy rumor. The witnesses, almost all the witnesses, say he was trying to save her."

"He was never arrested. Never charged. Is that because he works here?"

"There was nothing to charge him with, Ed."

"That right?"

"I'm sure he didn't hurt her. She was his beautiful prize student."

He said nothing, only looked at her as though to ask how she could think being beautiful and prized could keep someone safe.

"I'm glad she can be with her mother," Stack said then. "I don't need any ceremony. She wouldn't want it."

"Whatever you want," Jo said. "Whenever." It became apparent to her that he was very ill. He took an inhaler out of his jacket pocket and breathed from it. She asked if he had asthma. Emphysema, he said. Severe.

"You know what I'd like?" Stack said. "I'd like to see the street where it happened."

"Really?" Jo asked. She did not care for the idea.

"Yeah, I'd like to see the place."

It was not clear to Jo whether Stack knew that Maud had been struck in front of the Brookman house. In any case, his wanting to see it made her distinctly uneasy.

"Can you direct me? Jo Carr? That your name?"

"Call me Jo, Ed."

"Yeah," he said, "sure."

"I can show you the street if you want to see it."

She led him out of the office and toward the muddy Common, edged in banks of soiled melted snow. The first of the homeless people had assembled for lunch, lined up along the spiked fence of First Presbyterian's churchyard. Its carillon was sounding the Rose Carol.

Jo walked him around the Common and then started down Amity Street to Walnut and the hockey rink.

"You don't have to come with me, Miss Carr. Just show me the way."

"I don't mind," Jo said.

"I don't want you to come."

"Well," she said, "it's two blocks from here. If you turn left at the rink. On the right side of the street. Midway." He nodded his thanks and she watched him walk in the direction of the rink. He had bought a cheap drugstore cane that morning to support himself on the part of his journey that would have to be covered on foot. He did not really lean on it as he walked— rather, he swung it in front of him at shin level, almost like a blind man. Still, in his weakened state his progress was slow. Watching him, she wanted to call him back, interrupt whatever he thought he was doing.

"Ed!"

He turned slowly, reacting to his first name.

"You know where to find me, Ed!"

"Sure thing."

Back in the office, Jo found her end-of-term caretaking bogged down in petty details and worrisome distractions. The distraction that worried her most was the conversation she had just had with Edward Stack. That he had come to the college at all was disturbing, and she avoided the question of his visit during their exchange. Finally it worried her enough to phone Salmone at the police station and mention that she had seen Stack. She called Salmone rather than college security because she knew he had spent time with Stack in the NYPD. She also had a question for the lieutenant, the answer to which she hoped would allow her to rest easier.

"He asked me to direct him to the scene of his daughter's death," she said when she had Salmone on the line. "It seemed a reasonable thing. I guess I didn't put it all together in that moment. It being the Brookmans' house."

"Was he threatening? Was he agitated?"

"I didn't think so."

"Had he been drinking?"

"It occurred to me. I thought he might have been, but he wasn't acting very intoxicated and there wasn't a detectable booze aura there." A little cagey was how she thought of him later.

Salmone thanked her for the call.

"Lieutenant? Did you find out anything about the man I mentioned? The man who calls himself Father Walter?"

"Your guy is dead ten years, Dr. Carr."

"Is that certain?"

"Seems really certain. He was well known where he lived. Somewhere in Louisiana, as I remember. He died of cancer. Had it a long time."

"A man came to see me one evening. Livid about Maud's article. I would have sworn it was Walter. I knew him well. If someone asked me in court if I'd seen him, I would have sworn on the Bible this was the same man."

"Couldn't be, Dr. Carr. He was a well-known figure. Death's been established."

"You made a special inquiry?"

"Hey, we pushed those people so hard they think we're nuts. Your Father Walter is dead. No question."

When he had identified Brookman's house, Stack found a bench with a dedicatory plaque under a massive catalpa tree almost directly across the street from it. He was out of breath after his walk from the counseling office; the place to sit and the warm sun were welcome. The day was bright, the street fairly quiet since the students were away now and many of the buildings were closed. Around the Common, two blocks away, the hour was told in Christmas hymns by each church in turn.

As Stack settled against one end of the bench, the holstered Glock thudded against its armrest. He laid his cane down the length of the seat and read the plaque. The dedication was to

a professor and his wife whose favorite tree it had been, sub-
scribed to by former students after their deaths, sometime in
the 1930s. Nice world they lived in, he thought, but of course
it would not have seemed that way to them. Stack stretched his
embittered, whiskey-poisoned bones on the slats. So quiet was
it that he might listen to the twittering of riverside swallows
that had established themselves in the park shed's ornamental
eaves. Sitting here he could almost hear the impact that had
crushed the last living breath out of his only child along with
the skittering of the swallows and the earliest doves of afternoon, reporting into the quiet spaces.

At first Stack had cried over the violence of his daughter's
death. But the more he thought about it, the more it seemed
connected to his own fate and nature, and he cried no longer.
It took a certain kind of individual to wipe out a beauty like
Maud's. But she was only Stack's Maud and Stack was a thief
and Maud was another and they had thrived on loot. Was that
putting it too harshly?

It was all easy to understand. Stack the monster and the monster's lovely daughter — it was a rendering of justice against both
of them. Because she was Maud, the sometime thief, the spoiled
and selfish. Because she was his beautiful brilliant only child.
Because he loved her so much more than life. Because he and
her mother loved her so much.

As for himself, he thought, for all the gifts he might have
started with, he was a burnout and a drunk, not even a medio-

cre policeman, a lousy one in fact, and not a particularly honest
one. A coward, morally and sometimes physically. A spiteful,
vengeful nurser of old wounds, a bigot at heart, a rejoicer in the
defeats of others, a betrayer of his adoring wife as womanizer
and cuckold. An accessory to sometimes vicious things and to
crimes he lacked the stones to perpetrate or prevent.

It seemed to him he had been poisoned by anger long before
he had any right to it. It must be in his blood, he thought, the
anger. He had known honor and pretended to despise it, and
come in the end to really despise it, to dread hope, fear light,
laugh off all the dreams of justice, laugh it all off. Those were the
reasons she was dead.

Looking across the street from his bench, he saw a tall woman
in a tan raincoat coming up the street with her eyes on the sidewalk. She wore glasses, and a scarf was tied loosely around her
neck. With her was a girl of ten or so. The child drew Stack's
attention. She had darker hair than her mother and was at an
awkward age of her growth. Her wrists showed beyond the
sleeves of her ski jacket. She was tall and long-legged but her
face, with its high forehead, was dour, downright sad, the face
of a noticeably intelligent little girl. As they stopped in front of
the Brookman house her mother pulled her sleeve at the elbow,
reminding her that they were home. For a moment the woman
stood looking down at her daughter with concern, touching
her hair lightly, her face drawn with worry and unhappiness.
They would be Brookman's people, Stack decided, engaged in

the pleasures of parenting. In that moment Stack realized how different his life would be as the father of dead Maud.

The thought was fascinating. All gone. The wife, the daughter who had seemed magical and more as a child but had proved only surpassing in beauty and intellect, otherwise an ordinary mortal like himself. A man, Stack thought, who has a child like her believes it's himself transcended. But the Stacks of the world did not transcend. Still, she had surprised. Maud had been touched by something strong. She had surprised but the power of the *Sidhe*, the fairies who owned her, had brought her down. Head to head with religion, the kid had gone. How he had loved her!

He thought it the easiest thing in the world now, to understand. Some force overcome with rage like his own had demanded that miracle child of form and grace be crushed on the sidewalk like a roach. The life he was living since the day he made himself understand that his daughter was dead was different from the one he had lived before. It was compounded still of rage and grief — they were still present, still a scourge — only less confusing. He felt as if he suddenly commanded a clear view into what had been his life, and it seemed to be one where he had outlived identity. The papers he carried, for the weapon, the driver's license, all the credentials that defined him — even his own name — had no significance at all. Not that this brought any particular freedom. Freedom had always been a thing alien to him, as a concept or as an experienced condition. No one and nothing was free, everything rigorously bound and priced, locked down and chained, from your last drink to your last orgasm to what you thought were the highest flights of your soul. Stack was out of breath. He took his hat off and leaned on the cheap cane. It was late afternoon but the day was still bright. He was waiting for the courage to telephone Brookman in the house across the street.

He had been sitting a long time and the mild day concealed a chill at its core that worked its way into Stack's bones. He had taken to feeling the outline of his Glock as though time or reason had somehow stripped him of it. Finally, after the winter shadows had edged from one side of Felicity Street to the other, he saw a man he knew must be Brookman headed up the street. Brookman was a large man, a few inches over six feet tall, and the unbuttoned charcoal-gray overcoat he wore spoke for the breadth of his shoulders. He would have to be approached, as the term went, "with caution." He would have to be killed quickly and beyond a dying effort. Stack's hand went to the weapon under the cloth of his coat.

He watched as the man he knew was Brookman turned briskly into his elegant residence on Felicity Street. At the point of taking out his cell phone, Stack was at once aware of an unmarked car, a few years old, blocking traffic in the near lane. His friend Salmone was at the wheel and rolled down the passenger-side window.

"Hey, Eddie!"

Stack stood up. His instinct was to walk away.

"Eddie!" Salmone pushed open the passenger-side door. "Eddie. Step into my office, brother."

His capacity for escape was a thing of the past. Stack walked into the street and climbed into Salmone's Camry. They drove down the street that led to the center of the Common and parked in a row of spaces marked off for utility vehicles.

"Dr. Carr call you?" Stack asked.

"What are you doing in front of their house, Eddie?"

"I was meditating."

"Look, man. Somebody ran Maudie down and left her to die in the street. It wasn't Brookman, for Christ's sake. And everything we know is telling us now he didn't do anything like push her. His wife was there."

"His wife was there? Of course she's gonna fucking defend him."

"I'm thinking this woman is a lousy liar. Even in extreme situations. I'm thinking I'm gonna know when this babe is lying to me. What he says, what she says — it's corroborated. The early stuff was not reliable. Accusing witnesses didn't stand up at interviews, or they weren't really witnesses — they didn't see it."

"He seduced my daughter, Sal. He mocked us. He made her a whore."

Salmone shook his head.

"Don't talk like a meathead. I'm sorry, Eddie. Don't destroy your life. Her memory. Her mother's memory. Your own legacy."

"My legacy? What the fuck is my legacy? Legacy! Some

bullshit term of media correctness to perfume the shit people do? My old man could talk legacy, the Irish legacy on the docks, on the tugs. You want to talk Sicilian legacy, Sal? My legacy, my dick."

Salmone, offended and angry, sat silently for a moment and looked around to see if anyone outside was near enough to have heard.

"This got you where you got no pride, Eddie. I feel sorry for you. I got pride if you don't."

"I'm talkin' about myself, Sal. Not about anybody else."

"All right. Get a hold of yourself, for Christ's sake."

"I was a mooch, a jelly," Stack said. "You know what Kinsella said in front of me?"

Salmone folded his arms and raised his eyes.

"Don't, Eddie, for God's sake."

"He's talking, Charlie, about cops on the bag. He says some cops can take it and some can't. If you don't know how to take it, you shouldn't. He said, 'Some cops would love to take it but they don't know how.' He says this in front of Barbara. He was talking about me. And then, after the thing—"

"Shut up, Eddie!" Salmone shouted. "Shut the fuck up! You were honest as the day was fucking long. You were incorruptible and you were smart and everybody loved you and especially Barbara—she's a saint in heaven—she loved you. Kinsella's a piece of shit."

Salmone paused and considered his old partner. "Hey," he said, "are you carrying? Do you have a weapon?"

"No," Stack said.

"Look," Salmone said, "I blame myself. I didn't like Brookman. I was pissed. I swear I was pissed at his behavior. And because I knew who Maudie was. But he didn't push her in front of no car. I didn't say he did, did I? I was suspicious."

Stack watched the Christmas lights on Prospect Street switch on.

"I can tell you this too, Eddie. The Staties got a list of people reported their car stolen right after Maud died. Had work done on it. There's gonna be an arrest soon. So there's that." He turned to Stack. "Eh, I think you went crazy and I think you got a weapon. I want it."

Stack ignored him.

"You want to end up in the fuckin' zoo at the end of your life? You want to dishonor yourself so much?"

Stack shook his head.

"Or," Salmone said, "you want the garbage guys and the coroner sweeping up your fucking brains and the rest of your family thinking about that? And the sin."

"Oh, fuck the sin, Sal."

Salmone put his hand out. "I want the weapon. I'll get it to you. You want a receipt? I'll personally return it to you. Now I want it."

So in the end Stack handed over the Glock. Salmone looked at his watch.

"There's a train now every half hour. You're gonna make the four-twenty. I'll give you a ride."

"I don't want a ride," Stack said. But he took it.

At the station, on the platform, Stack watched the four-twenty pull away. He was not going to miss his appointment with Brookman, he thought, even if it was just an announcement of things future. He leaned on his cheap walking cane. He was having more and more trouble getting over the distances his routines required. Also, he thought, he might find a variety of uses for it. He took out his phone and called Professor Brookman's home.

36

"PROFESSOR BROOKMAN?"

He had never seen or heard Edward Stack, the bereaved, the famous cop, but he knew who it was.

"Yes?"

"Could I have a word with you? My name is Stack. I was Maud's father."

"I'm very sorry," Brookman said after a moment. He supposed there was no way around saying that. "You know we saw her just before she died."

Brookman did not understand what had impelled him to say it. His expensive new lawyer had been eloquent and specific on the sorts of things persons even potentially of interest in such a situation ought not to allow themselves to say. Say to anyone, let alone policemen who were members of the victim's immediate family.

"I know that, Professor," Stack said. "I thought it was time I reached out to you."

"I see."

"I think we should meet now," Stack said.

It was strange. Just as he had heard the outer-borough inflections in Maud's imitation of her father, so he heard Maud's shaped schoolgirl tones in her father's voice. It caused him a thrill of grief.

"If you would like to meet, Mr. Stack, I'll be pleased to meet you."

"That's good, man."

"You must have been," Brookman allowed himself to say, "very proud of her."

He listened to what sounded almost like deliberate heavy breathing on the phone. And Stack asked him:

"Why's that?"

Brookman felt an anger rise in himself that he could hardly keep out of his voice. It had been threatening to overwhelm him since the night of her death, along with the fear, regret, disgust.

"I'm sorry, Mr. Stack. Did you ask me why I think you must have been proud of Maud?"

"Yes," Stack said. "That is what I asked you."

"Because she was a wonderful young person. You must have known that better than anyone. Where shall we get together? When?"

"I'm in town, Professor. I'm in your town."

"Good," said Brookman. "Sorry I can't ask you to the house. How about meeting in my office? I can tell you where it is."

"I know where it is," Stack said. "Don't you want a public place?"

"I don't need a public place. Let's get together. Cortland 3A. The building's probably locked now but I'll open it."

He hung up and looked out his bedroom window at the early evening. Along the parkway that ran from the Common to the football stadium the commuter traffic was light and the three streetlights that marked the first two blocks were on. He turned on the bedside lamps and went out into the upstairs hallway. Ellie was down in the living room. Sophia was in the kitchen doing homework with Brahms on her CD player. It was the kind of music she did homework to. One of the many things that made her, among faculty brats, the arch-weirdo.

He called down to his wife. She came upstairs, grim-faced.

"Was that Stack?" she asked softly.

"Yes," he said. "How did you know?"

She shrugged.

"He's in town," Brookman told his wife. "He wants to meet me at the office. But he could be anywhere out there. Go down and lock up."

She started for the steps.

"Listen," he said to her. "I'm going up there. Lock up behind me and let nobody in here. No cop stuff or any such bullshit. Don't open it."

She nodded and went downstairs. Brookman went to a utility room at the end of the hall, locked himself in, turned on the light. It was the place he kept his outdoor equipment, his guns and fishing rods, his climbing gear, tents, protective clothing. One of the things he also kept there was a .38-caliber pistol, a few years old. He stuffed it in the wide pocket of an old parka and prepared to go out. When he switched off the utility room light there was a double knock at the room's door. He opened it to Ellie. He had put on the parka in the semi-darkness. Her hand found the gun's outline in his pocket.

"Steven! Don't meet him with that. It's wrong. It will destroy you. Destroy us." She was trying to keep her voice down. They both were.

"Of course I'm taking it," he told her. "He'll have one. While I'm out, you should load the Mossberg. The shells are on the shelf. Oil it and load it. I'm going."

"No," she said. "You mustn't!"

He seized her by the shoulder.

"Don't be a complete fool, Ellie. He means revenge. He thinks I killed his daughter. He's coming after us."

Brookman hurried out before Sophia had time to come out of the kitchen.

37

IT WAS ALMOST DARK when Brookman walked across the half-deserted campus to Cortland Hall. A river fog shrouded the brick college structures and reduced the town's Christmas decorations to a distant haze of holiday colors. The building's hallway lights were off; Brookman switched them on, left the outside door unlocked and went upstairs to his office. He left his office door unlocked as well and sat down behind his fine oak desk.

Maud had left her paperback *Doctor Faustus* and a plaid scarf on one of the captain's chairs with their emblazoned motto *Lux in umbras procedet*. Copies of the *Gazette* featuring her story were stacked in a rocking chair. For some reason there was a copy of *Smith's Recognizable Patterns of Human Malformation* on his sofa.

Brookman felt guilt and bitter regret but it was not any illusion of atonement that drove him to face her father. He had a sense of debt to the man and to his daughter's memory but he was not offering himself in reparation. For one thing, he wanted to draw Stack's anger away from his house and his family. But it was not remorse for the most part that moved him to face Stack. Other forces inside him, old determinants of his life and fortune, drove him. Two things were foremost in his mind: his family in the house down the hill and his shame at bringing the gun along.

He did not believe that he had killed Maud by loving her, through what had happened between them. Still, there was some kind of blood debt, something to be endured as a result of what had happened. He thought of it as something to be learned, a mystery he was compelled to live out. What brought him to the office and the meeting with Stack was akin to every other high-risk venture he had ever undertaken. Maybe the temptation of oblivion, or an obsessive curiosity about the ineluctability of fate. And an ancient anger he had been born with, an insatiable rage against himself, his cast of mind — a sense that he had been born out of line, raised wrong, lived deserving of some unknowable retribution that it was his duty and honor to face down, prevent, overcome. His yielding to the spell of Maud, the pain he had caused Ellie, his coming into the path of the unfortunate old man's revenge, all were mysteriously part of it.

He heard the outside door open slowly. When it shut, the building sounded with an echoing hush, the magnified whispery desperation of Stack's breathing, in discord with his footsteps and the reports of his cane against the oak floors.

Brookman sat silent and unmoving, frozen in place. In the office, he could detect a lingering savor of the girl that quickened on the thoughts of her he had spent so many days resisting. Somewhere at the center of the confusion and grief of the past weeks, he remained trapped in images from the teeming street in front of his house in the moments before the phantom car had struck. At his heart was a dreadful sense of loss, of life, of love, all lost, so wrongly, so unjustly, so in accordance with the wretched laws of life. Maud lost. And Ellie and Sophia — every loving impulse he knew, dead at the source, dead on arrival. Can I have brought down all this death in life on us, Brookman wondered, through my fondness for a pretty girl? And could Maud have been led to death through so commonplace an adolescent adventure? It was all so good, he thought, all about the beauty of a girl and of the world, of its forms, its sublimest language. He waited, despising his own fecklessness and self-pity yet offering them to fortune as his alibi. He thought of the Thomas Wyatt verse in her pocket. God have mercy on her.

When her loose gown from her shoulders did fall . . .

She carried it in her wallet, he thought. Carried it for me. God have mercy on her, he thought. On us, on me. How learned and fine we believed ourselves to be! How shitty of the world to deal with us this way.

The tapping of the old man's cane was harrowing him. Then there was the knock on his door, and it was a four-beat measure that reminded him of Maud's signal.

"Professor Brookman?"

"It's open, Mr. Stack."

He heard Stack pause for breath and cursed the impulses that had led him to wait seated at the desk like some lame victim of justice. He ought, he thought suddenly, to have stood by the door and taken the old guy down, weapon and all if he had one. Brookman grew angrier and angrier. In the hurried failing breaths of the man at his door he could sense the satisfaction of an avenger, and a sense of his own justification drove his rage. He put his hands on his desk and watched Stack come into his office.

Edward Stack looked to be a hard man with a practical cop's face. A man used to being feared. Maud had his eyes, Brookman thought; you would have paired the two of them by sight because of the eyes.

"You," Stack said. He did not say it in an agitated manner but softly, with an edge of satisfaction. It was an intimidating way to be addressed, but it fed Brookman's anger. As Stack said it, the cane fell from his hand, clattered on the wood floor and rolled across it. It was the kind of stick chain drugstores sold to aging cut-rate cripples. Both men looked down after it. Stack made no move to retrieve the thing.

"Were you going to hit me with that, Mr. Stack? Were you going to cane me?"

He watched the old man struggle for breath, not able after a moment to conceal his gasping.

"For God's sake," Brookman said.

Brookman stood, his eyes on Stack's, and came around the desk. Stack took a move back and put the right hand that had held his cane on the arm of the chair nearest Brookman's desk. It was there for students' use during office hours and Maud had sat in it often enough. Stack put his hands on the chair and eased himself into it, fighting for air.

Brookman saw that the old man had miscalculated. Whatever he had intended was beyond him, whatever havoc on Brookman he saw himself as wreaking in his mind's eye was well past his capacity. He was settling for life and breath, propped on the chair. There were no threatening motions, no reaches for weaponry. He did not even try to talk. At first he could not bring himself to look at Brookman, and when he did, he was attempting not to show the fear he plainly felt. Brookman was ashamed.

"Are you all right?" Brookman asked him, avoiding his eyes. "Do you want oxygen? Should I get help?"

"You son of a bitch," Stack said, breathing hard. "I came here to kill you."

"That would have been wrong, Mr. Stack."

Stack began to laugh. Brookman wanted to beg him to rest and be silent.

"We got to be friends over the years I was her adviser. I let it get out of hand. I was emotionally involved and she was ..." Something in Stack's expression made him stop.

"You ... you phony obscene son of a bitch. You ... bastard. She was a young child."

"No. She was my student, Mr. Stack. I always respected her. I let the distance between us become too close."

"Stop calling me that, you posturing fuck. Stop calling me Mr. Stack."

"Sorry. What shall I call you?"

Stack tossed his head in what looked like a spasm of pain.

"It sounds like you're passing yourself off as someone her age. You're a married man, you bastard. She was a child."

"Not to me."

"Like you were a couple of kids, you dirty-handed son of a whore."

"Two grown people."

"She was younger than her age," Stack said fiercely.

"She was a beautiful, educated young woman."

"Oh, bullshit. She was a kid!"

"She looked that way to you."

"You killed her, didn't you? That's what it comes to."

"She died in an accident."

"It wasn't an accident," Stack insisted. He sounded as though he knew he was arguing against logic.

"She died in an accident. It could have been anyone in that street. It could have been me." He leaned his forehead on the heel of one hand. His elbow touched the weight of the gun in his pocket and he was ashamed of having it. "It's so cruel," he said to Stack. "I'm sorry."

Stack stared at him wide-eyed, his handsome ravaged face ugly with animal suffocation and his hatred.

"But emotionally," Stack repeated, "she was younger than her age. She was a kid."

Without meaning to, Brookman shrugged. He sat silent, to let the old man catch his breath and because he did not know how to answer.

"You say cruel," Stack reminded him. "How about you for cruel? To crush a kid's feelings like that. Break her heart! You act like I don't understand. Like I don't know what you did." He coughed, took out his handkerchief, turned in the chair and folded his hands over the back of it.

A nice-looking man, Brookman thought, his adversary had been. But his basically lean, intelligent looks were utterly blasted, the fine eyes swollen, the fair skin flanneled and flayed, marred under his high cheekbones by sickening spidery angiomas.

"I saw your family, Professor," Stack said. "I bet they're good people. They weren't enough for you? Why didn't you leave us alone?"

"Maud was my friend and my student, Mr. Stack. I never, ever meant to hurt her. I respected her and I respect you. If you thought I was patronizing you, you were mistaken."

"You picked her up, you seduced her, and you dropped her, and you should not have done that. I swear to God I came here to kill you."

For that, Brookman had no answer. Only the pistol he was more and more ashamed of having.

He stood up, walked around the desk and picked up Stack's cane. Standing over Stack's chair, he offered him the handle. As he did, he realized that Stack had caught a glimpse of the gun in the right pocket of his parka. Stack struggled to his feet, reaching toward him, and Brookman gave him a shove that drove him toward the wall. The old man was wheezing, reaching for his inhaler. Brookman backed away. For a moment, he thought he might have killed him. But Stack caught his breath.

"You son of a bitch, Brookman!"

"Sorry about the weapon," Brookman said. "I didn't know what to expect. I didn't come up here to shoot you."

"Well, I'll tell you what, Professor. I got nothing to lose, Professor. You better think before you let me walk out of here. Because I'm gonna have it done. Too bad about your nice family. And maybe everything was the way you claim. But I'm gonna see you get done for what you did to me, and the people who are gonna do it know all about cruel. So you can give them your thoughtful reflections while they work."

After a moment he saw that Stack was laughing at him. Or pretending to. His eyes were alive, blazing with contempt that was altogether genuine.

"You conniving scumbag. You brought a weapon. You have a fucking piece on you!"

"I have a family too, Mr. Stack. The way things are . . . I mean, I didn't come up here to hurt you."

"No, you would have got fired, wouldn't you? No, Professor. I don't think I would have used a gun on you either. I'm too old and feeble to get myself arrested and locked down and endure all those fucking formalities over a piece of shit like you."

Brookman watched him and realized he was unarmed. "All that uncomfortable confinement in the shitty jail you people keep for your menials. Not me! I mean, the shame of it all? Over you? No way."

He thrust his fist against his palm, trying to act out a triumph he lacked the breath for.

"You should be in a hospital, Stack," Brookman told him. "Are you sure you can get home?"

"Let's see the pistol, cowboy. Let's see what you brought for me."

"I want you to leave, Stack. If you won't, I'll have to call security."

Stack stood up slowly.

"I'm so sorry," Brookman heard himself say. "I'm so sorry about what happened."

The old cop looked him over.

"You're really upset, aren't you? You're sorry. You're telling me you're sorry?"

Brookman only nodded.

"It was bad luck, right? Bad luck for everybody. Like a mistake."

"Yes. I guess so."

"Well, Professor Brookman," Stack said, "the people I'm sending to you have a saying. They say when somebody makes a mistake, somebody got to pay. So you're gonna pay. They'll explain — the people I'm sending. They like to talk, you like to talk, like to listen. So you'll understand."

"Get out," Brookman said.

"You know," said Stack, "you want to do the right thing, man, you should use that weapon. You should never let me walk out of here."

Brookman picked up the phone to call security. Stack went out before he finished dialing. Brookman supposed he himself had been bluffing, would never have completed the call. He replaced the receiver, sat down behind his desk under the faltering ceiling light and listened to Stack's footsteps and the tapping of his stick.

38

JO HAD LEFT HER CAR a block and a half down the street from the counseling office. Parking regulations for the upcoming weekend required her to move it to her designated college space. Crossing one intersection, she had a view of the central campus and Cortland Hall. All but one of the windows were dark and she wondered if the lighted one was Steve Brookman's. A minute later she saw Edward Stack heading her way on the far side of the street, advancing with the constricted gait of creeping suffocation. He guided and supported the weight of each right-footed step with the stick in his hand. Jo crossed the street to meet him.

"Hey," she said. "You stayed awhile."

"I stayed awhile," Stack said. "That's right."

His voice had the same sly diffidence she had heard in it hours before, a certain caginess with a touch of menace. But now he was breathing with difficulty, seizing breaths between words. His jaw was trembling too. As he leaned on the cane facing her, his whole body seemed touched by tremors and she could not

tell whether they reflected physical exhaustion or some emotional state. If Stack had walked all the way to Brookman's
house or to his office, he had covered a lot of ground for a man
in his condition. Had there been a confrontation? Had something passed between them? The first necessity, she thought,
was to get the old man off his feet.

"Bound for the station?" She looked at her watch. "You
missed the peak trains."

"Is that bad?"

"Well, you have a longer wait. Hey," she said, "let me give you
a ride."

"I was going to the taxi line."

"I'll tell you what. You can wait in my office, then I'll run you
over there and you won't have to sit around and catch pneumo-
nia in that place."

She saw that he was not in the mood to argue about a spot
of rest. She led him back to her office, turned on the lights and
showed him to the chair he had occupied earlier.

"So," Jo asked, "did you find the scene of the accident?"

He only nodded. Jo had no idea what to say or ask next. At
a loss, she thought, for follow-up questions like: How did you
like it? Would you consider endowing a memorial crosswalk?
Or for encouraging commentary like: We find people take comfort seeing the actual pavement. Isn't it a great campus? And
the building a block from where the car hit her was designed by
Stanford White. She nodded back. She was not so tough anymore, she thought. It was a close-run thing whether she would

break down and cry in front of him. He was going to die in grief, of grief. Was it too much to ask that he might have died rejoicing in his lovely daughter's prospective bright future? Proud of her youthful achievement? Apparently.

"Your COPD," she asked him. "Did you maybe respond on 9/11?"

She was trying to give him something to feel proud of but he looked at her more stricken than before.

"I saw Brookman," he said after a minute. "You must of called Lou Salmone."

It made her feel like a snitch. She had to remind herself not to be ashamed.

"Of course I did. I was afraid of the worst."

"I guess you did what you had to do. You were right to be afraid."

"I didn't know you saw him."

"Yeah. We talked."

"So what was that like?"

He shrugged her question off.

"I saw his wife and the young kid. I saw them go in the house."

"Nice people, Ed."

"I'm sure," he said.

"Listen," Jo told him. "Lots of people around here are smart, you can figure. Some people are invaluable to the world for how they use their intelligence. I know Ellie Brookman a little. Not everybody is like her. She's tops, Ed. All the way. She couldn't get hurt more than she has been. Nor have her child hurt. Be hurt through the child."

"He shouldn't pull the shit he does. With other women. With other people's kids."

"Of course he shouldn't. I think we have to suppose, perhaps, he fell in love. He never did anything to hurt her. Never meant to. He's childish, I guess."

"I've seen a lot of people go down being childish. And they went down in very bad ways over dumb shit. Being childish. Childish is no alibi with me."

"He's a risk taker," Jo said. "He doesn't mean harm. He had a pretty tough early life. He was an orphan. A guy can't get enough mama love. I don't know if you know what I mean."

"There's a lot of them like that."

"Ed," Jo said, "you got a right to do what you want, I guess. I mean, I don't really believe that, but where I come from and the places I been, I kind of believe that."

"Good," Stack said. "I'm glad somebody does. Good."

"But I have my hopes, you see. I have my hopes for pain — for pain cycles to stop somewhere. I've seen so much of it. A lot of people have seen a whole lot more but I feel like I've seen so much. I want to see this one stop somewhere."

"I wish I could promise you, but I can't. I can't promise you and I won't."

"I don't expect … I don't know about promises. I have my hopes. My hope is that you can take care of this for me."

He gave her no answer.

"OK," she said. "It's time for the train. Sit tight, I'll get the car."

Behind the wheel of her Taurus, she had the collapse. She could not make herself stop sobbing. Even screaming the convulsions down failed to stifle them.

"Shit, he's gonna miss his train," she finally told herself aloud.

She picked him up and they drove in silence to the station. It was quite a grand station. It might even, Jo thought, have been by Stanford White. Or Richardson, or McKim, one of those guys, if one of them had done railroad stations. Only this town, with its superbo college in it, would have a station like the Baths of Caracalla or the Baths of Nero or some such baths. She pulled up in front of the huge doors that were modeled on something in somebody's baths too. The latest wonder was that the place, after moldering for decades under industrial-strength filth, rust and pigeon shit, was actually clean.

Stack struggled out with his cane.

"I'll get out," she said. She turned off the ignition, though the cop in front of the station had spotted her illegal park and was on his way toward her.

"Don't," Stack said. He leaned down to face her at the open passenger-side door.

"I told your friend Brookman I was gonna get him whacked. I let him know — bad ways. He was gonna die."

Jo stared through the windshield, not seeing the outraged

cop who was remonstrating with them, brandishing a ticket pad.

"You can tell him it won't happen. Just . . . it won't happen."

"Because you're changing your mind?"

"Yeah. I'm changing my mind."

He started for the station doors, favoring the drugstore stick. The cop had stopped shouting at Jo. She seemed dreadfully upset, and he was afraid he had gone too far. Stack paused on his way into the station.

"It's all right," he told the officer. "It was life and death."

39

JO CARR HAD NO DIFFICULTY recognizing the contradictory impulses that the edifice of Holy Redeemer, as a suburban cathedral, had left unresolved. It had been built at a time when the liberalizing forces of the sixties were already being checked by embittered reaction. Plenty of the people who had moved their families from Manhattan or Brooklyn to the life of single-family, green-shuttered houses and tree-lined streets had seen enough of folk Masses and clerical protesters and girls on the altar assisting in the liturgy. The modernist design of the architect was being actively interfered with, as far as possible, by the newly promoted bishop and the forces created to empower the laity.

The white concrete exterior, enclosed by enormous aerodynamically curving buttresses, contained a huge amount of dark empty space. The gloom that in the old plan was meant to be dispelled by daylight had to be illuminated by outsize hanging lamps. The altar had been envisioned as a plain sacrificial block with minimal decoration but someone succeeded in adding a kind of reredos of gray concrete with statues of saints and the Virgin. Columns in support of nothing much went along the nave.

An old idea that had survived was the placement of crypts along the side aisles, and Barbara Stack's remains were contained in one of them. The urn was multicolored, an art nouveau vessel of a sort that Stack suspected only McCallum and Jenkins, of all the funeral directors in the neighborhood, would offer its customers. He had intended for Maud to choose Barbara's ciborium but decided finally that it would be too hard on her. Today they were putting Maud to rest in a similar urn, not the slate-colored casket but one with stones that recollected her black hair and blue eyes.

Jo Carr and Mary Pick had come down from Amesbury. Shelby Magoffin traveled from Manhattan via the most affordable limo service her current producers could find. She had been promoting her latest film at a press conference in a midtown hotel. Stack stood apart from them, facing the crypt, on which his own name and the names of his wife and daughter had now been lettered. *Edward Jeremiah Stack, Barbara Frances Stack* and *Maud Mary Stack*. He leaned on his drugstore walking stick and held his tweed Dannemora cap in his hand. Far from the mourners, near the church doors, stood Arthur Porgest, the sullen-looking assistant sexton, together with a large man in a tan windbreaker. Mary Pick had brought her cousin, an English priest visiting friends at Columbia University, who undertook the placing of Maud's remains behind the glass. The priest, named Wilfrid Pick, was a very tall man with disorderly red hair. His height allowed him to reach up to the crypt and manage Maud's interment without having to fully extend his arms.

Stack had all but forbidden prayers, but Father Pick presumed to recite the verses from 1 Corinthians about the stars differing from one another in glory, and the earthly body raised as a quickening spirit.

"May her soul and the souls of the faithful departed through the mercy of God rest in peace," he concluded.

Mary Pick said "Amen" and crossed herself.

"A shame about this place," Mary Pick said when they were outside. She and Jo and Eddie Stack shook hands and he put his cap on. He accepted a hug from Jo and from Mary Pick too. He shook hands with Father Pick.

"Can't we give you a lift, Ed?" Jo asked him.

"No. Thanks. Thanks, everybody."

Jo Carr and Mary Pick and Wilfrid Pick watched him go down the cathedral steps and stop a passing cab. Jo began to cry.

Coming out of the cathedral doors, Shelby saw that several photographers who had been at the press conference had found their way to Nassau County and were waiting on the steps. She could not help noticing that some represented an order of paparazzi a notch or two higher — at least in professional status — than the ones who had turned out for her in the past. In the pocket of her black raincoat she had brought a camera of her own, a tiny Polaroid with which to tease the photographers while they took her picture. Her revulsion for them was partly pretense; she did not find all photojournalists physically repellent. She understood that they had a living to make, and friends, relations and habits to support. On the other hand, her distaste was partly genuine, because they were frequently carrion feeders, thriving on the disaster and ruin of people who were often not unlike Shelby herself. The paparazzi on the church steps that afternoon presented themselves in that aspect.

Smiling agreeably, she walked toward her limo while the press corps — half a dozen young men and a couple of young women — skittered around her. One youth, expensively dressed down, pierced and tattooed at the gullet, stepped imperiously into her path, smiled back at her and totally impeded her passage. At once Shelby deployed her Polaroid.

"Miss Magoffin," the young fellow said, "do you fear for your life?"

In return she snapped his picture.

"Dude," she cried, handing him the shot, "if I had teeth like yours, I'd brush them."

All the photogs wailed piteously in unison, mocking her self-satisfied bitchiness. They'd all been there before. Shelby, by the time she felt able to let go, had forgotten the young journalists. Clustering around the car windows, they had the opportunity to see her cry and to take pictures of it too.

40

AFTER NEW YEAR'S A YOUNG woman from Taunton confessed to vehicular homicide in the case of Maud Stack. Lieutenant Salmone called Eddie on the phone. Stack's condition had declined, and though he did not bother to be abstemious in drink, his memory was intact.

"Woman," Salmone reported, "called Mona Carberry. White girl from Taunton, Mass. Twenty-seven years old. Single parent of a thirteen-month-old. Driving without insurance. History of minor traffic violations. Sometimes employed as a stripper. The car was her boyfriend's."

"Maybe he was driving?"

"We think maybe he was."

"God. Girls still do that?"

"Sometimes. You wouldn't believe. Guys do it for their girlfriends too."

"Jesus," Stack said. "There's hope for the world."

"You see it that way, Eddie?"

Stack grunted.

"They don't usually follow through on it if they're looking at time," Salmone said. "Just about never. So we think this guy will come forward pretty soon."

"Is there any connection with the article Maud wrote?"

"It doesn't look like it. The girl has no connection with the college, and besides, we think her boyfriend was the driver. He better come to his girlfriend's rescue soon or he'll be fucking sorry."

"Break him down," Stack said, "the dumb fuck. He doesn't deserve her."

"He was in Iraq. He got a Bronze Star. He has a drug arrest and a big pill problem. The girlfriend says he didn't want to go to the game so she went without him and got drunk. Doesn't sound very likely."

"No."

"Hey, listen, Eddie, how are you?"

"I'm lousy, Sal. But I'm old and sick."

"Right."

"I've lived too long already. Wouldn't you say?"

"It's not up to us, you know."

"Oh, fuck that, Sal. What are you giving me? Fucking religion. I'm tired of this. I'm trying to get pills. Something reliable. I don't like taking street shit."

"Sure, Eddie." Salmone disapproved. Man up, partner, he thought. Everybody dies. But of course not everyone has to lose a beautiful child.

"I'm gonna have to come for you and ask for my weapon back, Sal."

"Not from me you ain't getting it."

"I'm glad you took it, I really am. I might have wasted the fuck."

"You're not getting it back."

"I'd buy one, you know. I don't want to, though."

"That's good, Eddie. You don't need it, a guy like you."

"You know why I don't buy it?"

"Of course. You do it, you hurt other people. You hurt me."

"Let me tell you something. I don't worry about eating the gun or not. I worry about blasting some individual or other. I can take being remembered as a suicide. I don't want to go down as an asshole. The raging psycho."

"Don't hurt yourself, Eddie. Put it in the hands of God — like — you know, man. Don't hurt yourself anymore."

41

ONE DAY THE FOLLOWING SPRING, Steve Brookman was walking on the campus for almost the last time when he happened to meet John Spofford and Mary Pick in front of the college library.

Spofford, Brookman had been happy to learn, had not been fired after all. The decision to keep him on, Brookman thought, had been wise and just and not at all what Brookman might have expected from the college. The three of them stood in front of the library, the center of covert observation by many of the passersby. They agreed that Amesbury was a great place to be in April; it beat England any day, in spite of everything. People said more or less the same thing to each other every spring. Brookman was more than ready to subscribe to these ritual notions, aware that he expected to be six thousand miles away by the following April. Mary Pick was as cool as ever. Brookman and Spofford could not conceal their embarrassment.

When they were all saying what Brookman and Spofford

certainly hoped would be their ultimate goodbyes, Brookman gave him his hand and said, "*Semper fi.*"

"Yes," Spofford answered. "Right."

Immediately Brookman realized that the choice of words, in the circumstances, in the present company, was awkward. Spofford's attempt to disappear the phrase was no less so. It was very painful.

As the two men looked around for some route of withdrawal, Steve, John and Mary saw that a schizophrenic man often seen on campus — a man whose presence Brookman had noticed repeatedly in the weeks before the death of Maud Stack — was standing a few feet away from them. He was staring in something like terror at the three people who were blocking his path. As they hastened to step out of his way, the man uttered a sound, an anguished, fearful groan that seemed to emerge from somewhere inside him, somewhere so deep as to be incorporeal.

Mary Pick looked stricken, though Brookman thought she must have seen him often before. "Are you all right, dear," she said very sadly to the man.

He gave them a last terrified glance, turned around so that he was headed the opposite way and hurried off. The three stood silently for a while, watching him go.

42

ELSA BEZEIDENHOUT BROOKMAN TAUGHT HER advanced anthropology class until June. Her husband had contracted for a book on the Kamchatka Peninsula, and he went to Seattle to prepare for the trip. In July Ellie gave birth to another daughter, whom she and Steve named Rosalind after the witty heroine of *As You Like It*. Brookman came east but missed the event itself, which occurred a little earlier than expected. He was not displeased to be the parent of another daughter. They spent three weeks together before Brookman returned to his operational headquarters. After that, he came back at least once a month before suspending his field research. At the end of the year Ellie moved out of the house the Brookmans had occupied.

Ellie kept her job and, to the disapproval of many at the college, kept Brookman too. They planned to move to Boston, whence she would commute and where they were no longer a component of Amesbury's social scene. Steve worked on his book. Over time he grew steadily more obsessed with tigers and

planned more Siberian adventures, sometimes taking Ellie and
the children along.

Maud's death, and the degree to which his illusion of love for
Maud had been its occasion, filled him with remorse and regret.
What he suffered most acutely was the sense of his own unwor-
thiness, of the mediocrity into which life at the college, the
position and privilege of it, had led him. And Ellie demanded of
him something like a promise of connubial fidelity. Not in any
formula, utterance, whispered verse or knitted motto. Something worse, something that racked him with shame because it
forced him to understand that he had impelled a person such as
she was to ask such a thing of him, when what he owed her was
nothing less than the renewal of his moral existence.

It came to be that the love and admiration he felt for Ellie,
the strength he drew upon to feel like a worthwhile compan-
ion to her, were greater than any threat to what bound them
together. Something like the same thing was true on Ellie's side
as well. She was in fact a proud person who knew well what love
was. No one close to her had ever suspected her of not knowing
that. A woman with a sure sense of what she required in a man
and who put up with nothing out of mere fond regard. Endur-
ing each other's strengths, they survived something more for-
midable than serial adultery, jealousy or naive disillusionment.
Survive they did, though, and made do with arctic winters, with
watching the aurora and the proximity of tigers.

For a long time Brookman imagined that he had come away
intact from the things he had done and the things that had hap-

pened to him at the college. Then one day — a Siberian afternoon, while the trees in the forest around him crackled like
rifle shots as their branches contracted and a shadow seemed
to spread across the snow to darken it from soiled gray to nearly
black, Brookman found himself lost. He was on familiar ground.
The cabin he shared with Ellie could not have been half a mile
distant. But the lay of the land made no sense to him, and nothing clued him to direction. In the next moment he fell. The fall
was so violent it felt as though he had plunged downward from
a fair height, and he was breathless when his shoulder met the
frozen ground. When he tried to stand, the gloom around him
seemed to grow deeper than before. He heard the violent snap-
ping of the ice-bound limbs around him but there was not the
slightest rush of wind, only frozen stagnant silence encasing the
sounds. He had the sense there was a cat not far away.

Brookman's arm was stretched out on the dry dark snow and
he tried to turn it, elbow down, to get a purchase on the ground.
But as he labored, breathless now, to turn the arm one way, it
turned the other. The more force he brought to bear, gritting
his teeth, the more it rotated oppositely on the joint, leaving
him in agony. He stared down at the palm of his hand, the palm
he was trying to rise on. He shouted. Screamed was more like it.
The dark surrounding forest served to illuminate his shame.

Shame that he would never again elude. After that day's fall
the thought of what had happened would be a scourge to him as
it had not been before, and every step he took thereafter would
be edged with shadow. He had discovered the place to which

his own capacity for excusing himself, his self-indulgence, could not penetrate.

He did not die there in the pain and the cold as he expected but found his way to the cabin and to Ellie. Sleep failed him. His arm for weeks remained useless to him. He was, in a way, never the same again, though only he and Ellie would understand that.

When he went to the nearest doctor, at a gold mine forty kilometers away, the Russian medic there manipulated his elbow joint with a triumphant smirk. "Nothing wrong with your arm, dude." The Russians had lately taken to addressing people as "dude," especially Americans, who they thought had no business being around.

"It hurts like crazy," Brookman told him.

"Bummer," said the medical man.

He talked to Ellie about it as the use of his arm came back.

"Things like that come over me sometimes," she said. "Sort of fainting fits. I used to get them a lot when I was small. You must have caught it from me."

"It had a content, you know," he said. "That falling. It seemed to be about something. You know? Everything that happened at home."

"Sure," she said.

The driver of the car that had killed Maud Stack was a graduate of the college that fielded the visiting team for which his younger brother played. He was a decorated U.S. Army captain and a veteran of Desert Storm. Since his service, he had suffered problems with alcohol and pills. He had not wanted to go to the game. After the accident he had gone into a panic-driven fugue state and done all the dumb things—reported too late that his car was stolen, tried to do the body work on it himself, took it to a shop to attempt to conceal his own work. His girlfriend went to the police without his knowledge to confess to being the driver. When he found out, he walked into police headquarters and confessed to the crime. He had the court's sympathy but got a year inside.

The weather continued erratic in the months after Maud's death. Days dawned in murky spring-like warmth and turned frigid in the afternoons. Other days took opposite turns. On one of the cold mornings Jo drove down to a dead factory town called Old Brighton to see a psychiatrist friend of hers named Victor Lerner. Dr. Lerner was the son of a famous Hungarian therapist who had fled to Harvard during the Second World War. Victor had lost a coveted chair of his own by eloping with a student patient to an ashram in India run by his cultic mentor.

Since his dismissal Dr. Lerner had eventually regained his license and worked for the state on a contract basis. Most of his duty consisted in certifying applicants for disability benefits. He had an office out of which to conduct his sparse private practice, a crumbling nineteenth-century mansion that had belonged to an Old Brighton mill owner.

Jo Carr and Victor Lerner had been involved with radicals in South America, but in different parts of the continent. Their bond was that they had both attempted to subscribe to some of the totalist metaphysical fantasies that had thrived in the previous century. Jo occupied one of the rickety chairs facing his Goodwill Industries blond, maple-like desk. Across the dismal street behind him, visible through his office window, car after car of a freight train rattled by on the Boston & Maine tracks. The open cars carried stacks of empty wooden pallets secured by metal binders.

Victor and Jo had been talking about the death of Maud Stack. They had to suspend their conversation until the last freight car passed.

"And the dreams?"

"I dream about a place on the highest ridge of the Andes."

"You've been there before in dreams."

"Yes. And in the sky I see the stars. I see the constellation they call the Easel. Sacred in some places."

"How does that make you feel?"

She almost laughed. He had asked her the same question many times before. "It's a nightmare, Vic."

"And the associations . . ."

"A corner of something constant, a spirit deep in history. A created order. And all of the notions we've both seen people lose their lives to."

"Structuralist thinking," Victor said.

"I dream of that terrible priest. I see him on the street. He belongs to the rest of it."

"You don't need me to explain these things, Jo. You've already explained them to me."

"History ... history is poisoned by claims on underlying truth. We've both been burned by people who think they represent them. Underlying truth. Do you think any of these things are objectively out there?"

"Jo, on a scale of yes and no, I would have to say no. Counterintuitive as that may be."

"Why counterintuitive?"

"Ah," Victor said as another freight took sound and shape behind him. "Because people always want their suffering to mean something."

The rest of what he said was drowned out by the noise of the train.

Jo never stopped regretting that she had not been given more time to help old Stack somehow. How she might have found a friend in him, and of course whether she could have encouraged him toward survival. She had the feeling he might have been fun to know. As Maud would have been, Jo was sure, had the kid lived into knowability. And people had once considered Jo herself diverting company. Thinking about what she might have done for Stack, for Maud, helped her through the futilities of her job.

Stack died three months after his daughter. His ashes were placed with those of his wife and daughter in the crypt at Holy Redeemer.